Waterloo Station

ALSO BY EMILY GRAYSON

The Fountain
The Observatory
The Gazebo

Waterloo Station

A NOVEL

Emily Grayson

DOUBLEDAY LARGE PRINT HOME LIBRARY EDITION

WM

WILLIAM MORROW
An Imprint of HarperCollins*Publishers*

This Large Print Edition, prepared especially for Doubleday Large Print Home Library, contains the complete, unabridged text of the original Publisher's Edition.

WATERLOO STATION. Copyright © 2003 by Emily Grayson. All rights reserved. Printed in the United States of America. No part of this book may be used or reproduced in any manner whatsoever without written permission except in the case of brief quotations embodied in critical articles and reviews. For information address HarperCollins Publishers Inc., 10 East 53rd Street, New York, NY 10022.

ISBN 0-7394-3336-9

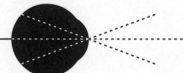

This Large Print Book carries the
Seal of Approval of N.A.V.H.

Waterloo Station

CHAPTER ONE

Though it's often said that old people possess a certain wisdom, Carrie Benedict suspected that her grandmother had been born wise. There was an uncommon intelligence in the elderly woman's eyes and words, a quality that seemed to have been there forever. So it was really not so unusual when, in the last days of the summer before she was to go off to college, Carrie Benedict chose to spend her final weekend in Longwood Falls, New York, helping her grandmother clean out her attic instead of choosing to go off with her boyfriend of six months, Rufus Cowley, a drummer in a local rock band, to an all-day picnic at the nearby falls. Rufus was astonished that Carrie had said no; they would be alone in a mossy grove, really alone, he'd told her, with a hamper of food and a cooler full of beer, and, of course, each other. What more could she possibly want? But Grandma Maude needed her this weekend, and that was that. Besides, Rufus could be demanding, calling the house several times a day, speaking to Carrie in his seductive, meandering cadences. They weren't in love, Carrie knew. Instead, at age eighteen, it seemed as though some sort of moondust had been tossed upon them, allowing them to enjoy their slow, tenuous time together, knowing it would most likely end when the summer did. When it came to the notion of actual *love,* the genuine article that she'd read about in magazines and had seen depicted floridly in movies, Carrie's attitude was one of doubt. Maybe, she thought, such love didn't even exist in the real world. Maybe what she felt for sweet, handsome, uninspiring Rufus was the most she could ever expect to feel for anyone.

Spending a day away from Rufus Cowley and these troubling questions was actually a bit of a relief to her. At 9 A.M. Carrie rang the doorbell of her grandmother's large, rambling yellow frame house on

Cheshire Road. Carrie's grandfather had recently died after a lingering struggle with cancer, and it was clear that Maude could no longer stay on alone in the house; there was too much for her to take care of—a roof that leaked in the lightest rain, and a temperamental plumbing system—not to mention the fact that Maude was frail. If she fell, who would know? Carrie's parents had discussed the matter at length and had finally convinced Maude to come and live with them. Which she was about to do, as soon as Carrie went off to college in a week. But before then, a formidable task needed to be accomplished, for Grandma Maude's house was like some kind of wild, overgrown museum in which nothing has been cataloged correctly, but everything, somehow, has been preserved.

When Carrie was small, she had loved coming to stay overnight in her grandparents' house. There were collections of snow globes and miniature doll furniture and post cards from just about every capital city of the world she could think of, as well as beautiful paintings on the walls, with their own little lights that illuminated the canvases. Her grandparents weren't collectors, exactly, and had never made a single purchase for investment reasons, but simply because they liked the looks of a painting or a knickknack on a table at someone's yard sale. Now Carrie's grandfather was gone, and her grandmother was suffering greatly. It had been three months since he'd passed away, but probably it only felt like three hours to Grandma Maude. She was a woman who felt everything deeply, freshly, nearly unbearably, it seemed at times. Carrie, at age eighteen, shared this trait with her.

"Come in, come in," said Maude at the screen door, and she kissed her granddaughter with great affection. "You are such an admirable person to spend the weekend with a creaky old thing like me, when you could be off doing dangerous and reckless teenage things instead."

Carrie laughed. "Personally, I think danger and recklessness are way overrated," she said.

"I certainly can't give you much in the way of excitement around here," Maude said, "though I *can* promise you some cheddar cheese sandwiches on toast and an icebox cake. That is," she added slyly, "if you do enough work for me."

"Sounds like a reasonable bribe," Carrie said, and she walked into the cool front hallway of her grandmother's house.

At age eighty-one, Maude was fragile but beautiful, with a head of striking white hair that she pulled back off her face in a single, slightly bohemian braid. Still, a few strands managed to float out, perennially giving her the appearance of someone in a hurry, someone who's been dashing somewhere and is afraid she's going to be late. These days, though, she had nowhere to dash to. She stayed in the house most of the time, mourning its imminent loss and still mourning the loss of her husband, unable to find any real interests with which to keep herself occupied. Friends called, inviting Maude out to dinner at one of the local restaurants, or to be a fourth hand in a card game, or to go see a movie, but she always said no, that she didn't have the time, or the energy, or *something.* Yet the task of going through an entire lifetime's worth of memories this weekend, poring over all the objects that she had once held so dear, had given her a new liveliness, and as Carrie followed her grandmother up the wide front stairs and along the hallway to a smaller set of stairs that led to the attic, Carrie had to struggle to keep up.

Unlike the rest of the house, which kept an ideal temperature throughout the summer months, the attic was broiling hot on this August day, but soon she and her grandmother had turned on an ancient fan, its dusty blades churning and cooling the air, and then the room became more tolerable. Carrie and her grandmother settled back on low stools in the middle of the attic, in front of an enormous steamer trunk. "I thought we'd start here," Maude said.

"What a beautiful trunk!" Carrie exclaimed. "I don't think I've seen it before, have I?"

"Well," said her grandmother, "it used to have a silk Japanese cloth lying across it, so I guess you couldn't really see what was underneath. But when I knew you were coming to help me today, I came up here and started to get things ready. And I knew the first thing I'd want to do was go through this old trunk."

Carrie ran her fingers across the rough,

corrugated leather surface. It was a black-ish brown, mottled color, its metal clasps completely gone to rust. There were labels pasted all over the trunk, too; some were difficult to read, but she could vaguely make out one of them: NEW YORK TO SOUTH-AMPTON.

"Was this yours?" she asked.

"It's been a very long time since I first used it," said Maude quietly. "Many, many years."

"How many, exactly?" Carrie asked gently.

"Let's see now," her grandmother said. Doing a little math in her head, she then replied, "Sixty-three."

"Sixty-three," said Carrie quietly. "That's an amazing amount of time."

But, truthfully, Carrie Benedict couldn't really imagine what sixty-three years would even feel like. The eighteen years she'd been alive so far had felt glacially slow, all of it building up and gathering momentum and leading toward her departure for college in a week. Sixty-three years ago, her grandmother had been a different person entirely. Her white head of hair had been reddish blonde, like Carrie's hair, and her colossal steamer trunk had been spanking new, its leather sides a pale doe-brown color, its brass hinges and clasps gleaming and catching the light. The entire *world* had been different, too, of course, though no matter how many history textbooks that Carrie, a top student, had managed to read over the course of her education at the hands of the Longwood Falls public schools, she still wasn't sure she under-stood what life had really been like back then. Sixty-three years ago would have been . . . Carrie was slower with the math than her grandmother . . . 1938.

1938! That was practically the dawn of civilization. The United States was in the throes of the Depression, and World War II was still a year away from arriving, though its seeds had already been planted throughout the continent of Europe. And then Carrie realized that in 1938, her grandmother would have been exactly the age that Carrie was now.

"You were eighteen then, like me," she said with wonder.

"Yes, I suppose I was," said Maude. "And now I'm eighty-one; the numerals are reversed. Eighteen and eighty-one; you're just starting out in your life, and me, well, I'm preparing to finish mine up."

"Don't say that," Carrie quickly said. "You could live twenty more years, Grandma, even more."

"Well, I can't say that I want to," said Maude softly.

There was silence between the two women. "But I *want* you to want to," Carrie said plaintively.

"I'm afraid it doesn't work that way," her grandmother said, shaking her head, and there was a moment of contemplative sadness in the air, which her grandmother quickly brushed aside by saying, "Well, enough of this weeping willow nonsense. We've got a lot of work to do today, you and I, if you plan on earning your sandwiches and cake later. Here," she said, "would you give me a hand?"

Together, the two women worked at the old, resistant hinges of the steamer trunk and finally managed to lift the cover from its mooring. Maybe this is what they mean by *steamer*, Carrie thought as a curtain of dust so thick it could have been steam swirled upward. Both women recoiled, coughing first and then, eventually, laughing.

"My God," said Maude. "I didn't realize this would asphyxiate us too. There must be a gas mask around here somewhere. We'll probably need it before the day's out."

"Did you really have a gas mask?" asked Carrie.

"Oh, certainly," said her grandmother. "We all did, back then, where I lived, in case Hitler dropped a bomb on us. I probably saved it over the years, just like I saved everything. Your grandfather always hated what a pack rat I am," she said. "He was perfectly happy to throw almost everything away. Said it was important that we be 'economical with space.' That was how he always put it."

Though her grandmother wasn't crying, something made Carrie reach out and impulsively hug her, and her grandmother hugged her back. Carrie could feel how small and delicate she seemed, like a dancer, or a china doll, or something breakable, and she could smell the clean fragrance of the lavender soap her grandmother always used; it mingled with the scent of something indefinable that simply represented who her grandmother was, and perhaps had always been.

"Thank you, darling," Maude said after they'd pulled back and were sitting quietly together. "I think I needed that. I'm just being a ridiculous old woman today, getting all caught up in a bunch of memories."

"No you're not," said Carrie. "You aren't ridiculous in the least." She wanted to say: *I think you're brilliant and wise, so please tell me how to live my life, how to know why it is I don't love Rufus Cowley and whether I'll ever love anyone.* But she held her tongue. Her grandmother had never had any real use for compliments, nor did she currently need the burden of helping an eighteen-year-old girl through her romantic worries. Carrie was here today only to help sort through a lifetime of objects, some of them pointless and discardable, others immeasurably valuable, if only to their owner. Telling the difference would prove to be the challenge.

Carrie reached into the trunk and pulled out an ancient, bulky, rusted metallic item that, at first, was entirely unrecognizable to her. "A . . . flashlight?" she finally asked hesitantly, and her grandmother nodded.

"Very good, Carrie," she said. "I'm impressed. Just look at this old thing. We called them 'torches,' back then, you know. This one is very heavy. I can't believe I used to haul it around with me."

"Should we save it?" Carrie asked, but her grandmother shook her head and said it was perfectly fine to throw it away.

"I'll feel a slight twinge," Maude explained. "But it's nothing I can't tolerate."

So Carrie, impressed at her grandmother's surprising ability to let go, dropped the ancient flashlight into a box marked DISCARD. The next thing she pulled out of the trunk was a page from a newspaper, completely yellowed and flaking, as though it were made of phyllo dough. On the page was a crossword puzzle, and its grid was entirely filled in with an ink that had turned pale blue over time. "How about this?" she asked.

Grandma Maude lifted her reading glasses, which hung on a silk rope around her neck, up onto the bridge of her nose. "Oh, would you look at that," she said quietly, shaking her head and peering intently at the old newspaper.

"I gather that this puzzle has some particular meaning," Carrie said. "Would you care to enlighten the rest of the people in the room?"

"I will," said Maude. "I will."

"Save it or throw it away?" asked Carrie.

Her grandmother took in a breath and then in a soft, uncertain voice said, "Oh . . . throw it away."

"Are you sure?"

"Yes," she said, nodding. "I am. This crossword puzzle does have a great deal of meaning for me—more than you can imagine—but it's no use holding on to it forever and letting it become clutter for other people to have to deal with. No, I think I can part with it. It already exists for me in here." Her grandmother tapped her forehead. "And in here." Then she tapped her heart.

It was two hours later, having sifted through all kinds of oddities, from tram tickets to stuffed animals, when Carrie Benedict pulled an old book from the very bottom of the steamer trunk. The book gave off a strong, musty smell, as though it had been lying in the woods for many decades. On the cover, though it had become severely compromised with age, Carrie could make out the words *The Poems of A. L. Slayton.*

"Who's A. L. Slayton?" she asked. "I don't think I've ever heard of him."

Her grandmother didn't answer at first. And when Carrie looked up at her, she saw that the old woman's eyes were bright with tears. Her hand shook as she reached out to take the book.

"Oh," was all Maude said in a voice so hushed that Carrie could barely hear it. "You've found it." And then she clutched the book against her chest.

"So I assume," said Carrie slowly, "that this book *doesn't* get thrown away?"

"No," said her grandmother, shaking her head. "Never." And then she very carefully opened it. It made a creaking sound, as though it were an old door. The pages were crisp and flaking, just like the newspaper had been, but her touch was gentle, and she quickly found the page she was looking for.

"There's a story behind this book," she said to her granddaughter, "and I'd very much like to tell it to you. It's a story about your grandfather and me."

"Of how you fell in love?" asked Carrie, thinking fleetingly of Rufus, and her own tempered feelings for him.

"Oh, that's certainly part of it," her grandmother said. "But it's also about much more than that. It all happened a very long time ago, as you can see from the dreadful shape this book is in. In fact, I don't know who's the worse for wear, me or this book."

"I'd very much like to hear the story," Carrie said.

Her grandmother smiled. "All right then," she said. "I'll start at the beginning."

"The beginning of your relationship?"

"Goodness, no. Before that. The beginning of my *awakening,* I think you could call it. The beginning of the time when I woke up from eighteen years of hibernation, eighteen years of living here in Longwood Falls with my parents and just doing what they told me, trying to be good all the time, never really thinking for myself. The beginning," she said, "of my *life,* I guess. Which started when I was your age." She took a breath, and then said, softly, "Nineteen thirty-eight."

CHAPTER TWO

It was inevitable that Maude Latham should have traveled across the Atlantic Ocean late that summer and ended up spending much of her life on the other side. She'd always been restless and impatient; it had started in childhood, when somehow all the games of capture the flag and hide-and-seek seemed to grow dull more quickly for her than for anyone else. She'd wander off right in the middle of a game, and her younger brother or sister would say, "Where's Maude going?"

The thing was, she didn't know where she was going, only that she wanted to go somewhere. And so, in August of 1938, her parents both cried softly into handkerchiefs as they saw their oldest child off onto the *Queen Mary,* which was docked in

New York Harbor. The ship was impossibly enormous and sleek; travelers streamed up the gangway, everyone waving, calling, feeling festive. On the dock, an accordionist played a jaunty version of "London Bridge," but if there was any festivity among the Latham family, no one would have known from just looking at them.

"You sure you know what you're doing?" Maude's father, Arthur Latham, asked quietly, pulling his daughter aside while her mother busied herself with the necessary tags for the steamer trunk.

He wasn't a very expressive man, spending his days among the incessant chatter of the looms at the textile mill he ran in Longwood Falls, and who could ever get a word in edgewise at home? But he loved his oldest daughter in a way that was different from his love for Ruthie or James. Not only was Maude restless, but she was also packed with ideas; they seemed to overflow from her, to keep her awake at night. She was a bookish but radiant girl; why keep her down? Maude Latham, everyone knew, would really go somewhere, would do something with her life, if she had the chance. Like her father, she was brainy and had a good heart, but unlike him, she wouldn't be content settling in the town where Lathams had lived for generations, scenic and lovely though it was. Still, Europe was a tinderbox right now, the newspapers warned in boldface, and all American travelers abroad needed to be aware of the fact that war could erupt at any minute. But surely England, where Maude was headed, was safe from Germany's bullying antics; surely stately old England was inviolable.

This, at least, was what Arthur Latham allowed himself to believe when against his better judgment he agreed to let his eighteen-year-old daughter attend Oxford University. No one in the Latham family had ever attended Oxford; no one, in fact, had ever attended college before. Despite the floundering economy, Arthur Latham remained a successful businessman whose fabrics were sold all over the United States. Even given financial success, he was sorry that he'd never had a good education, and no matter how many books he read over the course of his life (and he read books constantly) it could never make up for the deficit. *Deficit.* That was the way he

would always think. He was a businessman, not a scholar, and that would never
change. But his daughter could become a
scholar; she had a chance for an extraordinary life of the mind.

On her own, Maude applied to the famous, elite university, filling out all the required forms and then traveling by train
down to New York City on her own so she
could be interviewed at the Plaza Hotel by
a panel of ancient, visiting Oxford trustees,
who asked her a variety of questions in
British accents so thick that she was con-
tinually saying, "Pardon?"

"I said, 'Why do you want to attend Oxford, my dear gull?' " one man with a white
beard and rimless spectacles asked her
that day.

Maude paused. All eyes were upon her.
Another old man sipped sherry from a cut-
glass goblet; still another silently blew his
nose. All of them were waiting for her to
speak. *Why?* It was a reasonable question
he'd asked, but how could she possibly
explain what was in her heart, and what
had been there practically since she was
born? "Because," she finally said, "I want
to know the world."

Three months later, Maude Latham received her letter in the mail telling her she had been accepted to study literature at St. Hilda's College of the University of Oxford, one of the few women's colleges at this formerly all-male bastion. And now, on this broiling day in August, she stood on the dock at New York Harbor with her parents and brother and sister and a steamer trunk that, when it was stood on its end, was taller than she was. Her father had asked her if she was sure she knew what she was doing, and the answer, honestly, was no. She had no idea what she was doing, really; only that she had to do it. But she couldn't worry her father like that, and so Maude nodded briskly and said, "Of course I do." Then she hugged each of her family members in succession, ending with her father, whose tears made her feel as though her own heart was breaking.

"You won't forget about us, will you?" her little brother, James, suddenly asked.

"Of course I won't," Maude said in a voice that was meant to be dismissive, but the question almost put her over the edge, almost made her change her mind about going. Enough of this, Maude told herself sternly, and she extricated herself from the loving but tight grip of her family and climbed the metal stairs.

Now, one month later, she'd settled in fairly well at Oxford, this beautiful university located in its idyllic town with winding streets surrounded by the Hinksey Hills and the Thames and Gloucester Green with its clusters of double-decker buses, though it had taken her some time to learn all the rules and regulations: when the college gown had to be worn, when it didn't, which traditional Oxford ceremonies she needed to attend, what she was supposed to call her professors, who were known here not as professors but as "tutors." St. Hilda's, like all the women's colleges at the university, was a bit of an underdog. The real focus and fuss was on the men, and the women students were merely tolerated. Back in 1884, during a sermon given at New College, Dean Burgon had told the women in the congregation that "inferior to us God made you, and inferior to the end of time you will remain."

Things had changed somewhat by 1938, but not nearly enough, and yet the women at St. Hilda's soldiered on, spending late nights in the mausoleumlike library at St. Hilda's, heading into town in clusters before curfew to a tavern called The Bear, where they would meet up for pints of ale with some men they knew from Balliol College. The Bear was famous for its collection of interesting neckties, which were mounted in glass cases and displayed around the pub, though most of the customers quickly grew too drunk to pay close attention to any of them.

Maude's closest friend at Oxford, whose rooms were located down the corridor from her own, was an English girl named Edith Barrow. Edith was from a wealthy family in Devonshire, and she was in love with an upperclassman from Balliol by the name of Ned Waterstone; at The Bear one night the two lovebirds sat close together, their bodies touching at as many points as possible, while Maude sat across from them, trying to ignore the public display of affection as best she could, for it made her slightly uneasy. She'd never been in love before, and it irritated her that Edith would devote so much time and energy to romance when there was so much academic work to get done.

"Listen, Maude," said Ned suddenly, "a fellow I know name of Geoff Charter wanted to know if Edith had a girlfriend who could come along to his party Saturday night at the Swyndlestock."

"Do say yes," urged Edith. "There are always plenty of theatrical types there, Maude; it will be fun."

"You ought to go out with young men while you can, you know, Maude," said Ned.

"What do you mean, 'while she can'?" asked Edith, poking Ned lightly in the chest.

"Well, all the young men might be dead pretty soon, if things heat up with Germany," he said. "She'll have to go out on dates with the elderly and the infirm."

There was silence for a moment. "Don't be idiotic, Ned," Edith said, but her tone of voice had changed; it had a slight strain to it now. "That's a terrible thing to say," she added. "None of you men are going to be dead. I won't let it happen."

"Ah, you'll personally take care of me if there's a war?" Ned asked in a teasing tone. "You'll keep me from enlisting?"

"Absolutely," said Edith.

"Well, I'm afraid you won't have much luck," he went on. "If England gets into this business, then I'm joining the RAF. I've always wanted to fly."

"Look, there's *not* going to be a war," Edith said tensely. "And can we please talk about something else?"

So they turned back to talking about Ned's friend Geoff Charter again, and they tried to convince Maude to come to the party at the Swyndlestock, but she begged off, said she had to study, that she was falling behind in her Romantic Poetry tutorial. The truth was, Maude didn't really enjoy her evenings out in the city of Oxford. The university men seemed to her to be very full of themselves, extraordinarily conceited and certain of their own importance in the world. It was true that here were a future generation of barristers, members of parliament, and probably even a prime minister or two, but even so, their voices had begun to come together in an English upper-crust drone that she found infinitely annoying.

What was she looking for? Not love, certainly. Love wasn't something you reached out toward; it had to reach out toward you.

And though her friend Edith had found it so easily, or else it had found *her,* Maude didn't imagine that she would experience such a phenomenon herself. That wasn't why she had come to Oxford. She had come here to "know the world," as she'd told that panel of trustees back in New York.

It hadn't occurred to Maude Latham that "knowing the world" might mean what it ended up meaning. *Stephen.* It was Stephen who changed everything for her.

She had met him in late fall, when her Romantic poetry tutor, the elderly, fumbling Dr. Robertson, took ill with influenza and had to be hospitalized. It soon became clear that he was too ill to return to his tutorials for the rest of the year. In his place was a very different sort of man. For one thing, Stephen Kendall was surprisingly young, twenty-seven years old as it turned out, a lean, compact man with wavy, light brown hair and a shy, disarming smile. He wore his Oxford don's robes with a combination of irony and respectful accommodation to history. While the Romantic poets had seemed dull under Dr. Robertson's tutelage, they now came alive for Maude when discussed so intensely by Stephen Kendall.

Student and tutor sat together on soft chairs side by side in his study, a simple room lined with books. There was a wide oak desk with a photograph of a woman on it in a silver frame. The woman was beautiful; clearly she was Mrs. Kendall, though of course he never mentioned her. Dr. Kendall offered Maude a sherry, but she declined.

"Actually, I don't like the stuff much myself," he admitted with a shrug. "But when I was an undergraduate here, my tutors were always offering me sherry, and so by habit I guess I'm offering it to you."

"Well, thank you," said Maude suddenly, earnestly.

"You're welcome."

"No, not for the sherry."

"Then for what?" he asked.

"For treating me just like another student," she said. "Not like 'a female student,' the way some of the other tutors do around here."

"What do you mean?" Dr. Kendall asked, curious.

"I mean that very often at Oxford I feel as

though I'm being condescended to," said Maude. "As though I'm being *indulged.* My history tutor behaves that way all the time, calling me *Miss* in a very exaggerated tone of voice, and talking about the glory days of Oxford, when there were no women on the premises. But you seem to show absolutely no awareness of the fact that I'm a girl, and for that, well, I'm very grateful."

"Oh. I see," said Stephen Kendall, and then he blushed. The blush started under his collar and worked its way up, showing that not only was he a tutor, a young Oxford don, but also a person of the male persuasion who, despite what Maude had just said, *had* in fact noticed that she was a girl.

"Well," said Maude, smiling, "maybe you *have* noticed."

"Maybe I have," said Stephen Kendall, and then he blushed again. Quickly he turned back to the book of poetry before them, which was a volume of Shelley and Wordsworth and Maude's favorite, the tragic young Keats, but also included some of the lesser-known poets of that same era, such as A. L. Slayton, whose work Maude only vaguely knew.

Stephen Kendall had written his own Oxford thesis on Slayton's love poetry, and now he was introducing the work to Maude. Together, in the afternoon light, the two heads bent over the book. "Let's take a look," he said in his soft, slightly husky voice, "and see what good old Slayton has to tell us."

The tutor's hands were long and slender, Maude noticed as he turned the pages of the well-worn volume. On his ring finger was a wedding band; it was unpolished, as though he didn't take care of it, didn't really pay attention to its presence on his hand. Or else it was as though his love for his beautiful wife was so profound that the ring was treated only as the most casual of symbols, their love impossible to be fully represented by a narrow band of soft metal. She was daydreaming, she realized, and so she quickly turned back to her work.

One of the first poems by Slayton that they read together was called "The Rose and the Stag," and studying it with Stephen Kendall made Maude learn to love the long, intricate poem, and its author too,

who had died very young of tuberculosis.
The poem began like this:

> When first he happen'd upon her in
>   darkness,
> he found but a creature of God
>   unfinished, a
> project vague of intent, a lamp-lighter,
>   mild
> Her small hand reach'd out to waken
>   the wick with flame
> And he saw her eyes were wild . . .

Subsequent verses detailed the relationship between the man, a shipbuilder
known as "the stag," and the woman, a
lamp-lighter known as "the rose." Though
the poem has a happy ending, and the
characters do in fact end up spending the
rest of their lives together, in the very last
verse the rose has a terrible dream, a
nightmare in which the stag has left her:

> Her lamp was still lit but he no longer
>   saw,
> For he had chang'd o'er winter, the
>   way all stags do,
> hardening in the wild.

And she was flower to him no more,
but mere woman, imperfect.
She could not believe he could be so
  cruel.
Yet he left her there, a rose for all
  eternity,
then turn'd and leapt away.

"But why does Slayton give her that aw-ful dream?" Maude asked Stephen when he was done reading the poem in its en-tirety. "She's got everything she wants now, and they're both so happy with each other. Why must their happiness be tainted like that?"

"I think," said Stephen, "that even when genuine happiness actually occurs, one might fear it could be taken away. But you're right, they *are* happy at the end. It's completely real. Slayton is telling us that the rose will always have her anxieties about them, but that despite these worries, the two lovers will be together for eternity."

Stephen Kendall had read the whole poem aloud to her, all the stanzas, and his voice made it come to life immediately. It was as though, Maude thought, leaning back against the maroon leather cushion and looking at her tutor in the light that came through the leaded-glass windows of his study, he had experienced a similar love. How could he speak so movingly of romantic love if he hadn't? She became convinced that Stephen Kendall had a marriage of perfection, and that his wife was someone very much like himself: young, beautiful, tender. It was all she wished for him, Maude realized, and all she wished for herself one day. Why else marry if not for absolute, consuming love?

Her parents loved each other deeply, she knew, although they were very private about it, barely even touching hands in front of their three children. But once, years ago, she had accidentally come upon them in the parlor one evening. Her father held the palm of his hand flat against Maude's mother's cheek, and to this day she remembered what he had said to her: "Oh my love, just look at you." And her mother turned her head slightly to kiss his palm. Maude had been startled by this private display; like objects seen beneath the powerful lens of a microscope, entire worlds of love streamed beneath the surface of visible life.

Throughout that first long year at Oxford, Maude thought about her poetry tutor much of the time, not just during their tutorials, but even when she was supposed to be studying with her Latin tutor, a stick-shaped woman named, curiously, Dr. Wood, and when she gathered with other students at Skit Night and Follies Night and for dinner in the great dining hall of St. Hilda's, where the female students were served their meals from steaming tureens by a fleet of grim-faced female servants, and the fragrances of shepherd's pie and scotch broth rose up to the cathedral-high ceilings from which the chandeliers hung with their hundreds of little lights. She thought about Stephen Kendall all winter, which lasted almost unendurably month after month, wrapping the entire university and its surrounding town—the winding, narrow streets with their little tea shops and shoe shops, the Wolvercote paper mill, the Magdalen Bridge, the great river in the distance—in snow and ice.

Maude may have been a brilliant girl, but she was absolutely dense when it came to her feelings for Stephen Kendall. She thought she *admired* him. Admiration: that was the first word that came to mind. But one afternoon late that winter, when Maude was sitting in a bay window of her friend Edith's rooms while writing a composition, a fresh fire snapping behind the grate and Mrs. Salton, the charwoman, silently straightening up the mess of papers and books that Edith had so carelessly left all around her, Edith suddenly said, "You're madly in love with him, you know."

"Who?" asked Maude, for she genuinely had no idea of who Edith was talking about. Immediately her mind went to the various boys who traveled in their midst: Thom Leacock from Christ Church? Freddy Buckman from Merton College? She had absolutely no interest in either of them—Thom with his endless stories of cruel schoolboy life at the Dragon School, and Freddy with his supposedly ribald (but actually boring) slew of jokes.

"You know," Edith said, smiling slyly and offering Maude a glass of port.

"No, I really don't know," said Maude, shaking her head no at the port. "I'm afraid you'll have to tell me."

"Your *poetry* tutor," said Edith. "Kendall.

I've never heard another student jabber on as much about one particular tutor as you do about him."

"I'm *not* in love with him, Edith," Maude quickly said, "I'm simply in love with *poetry,* and he's the vessel, don't you understand? Stephen Kendall is a married man, and I'm offended that you would suggest my interest in him is anything other than purely academic."

"The lady doth protest too much, methinks" was all Edith Barrow would say.

Then Maude suddenly accepted that glass of port after all, downing the amber liquid in one hard swallow that first cooled her, then warmed her, then left her feeling as though her head might catch fire and explode. It wasn't *possible* that she was in love with Stephen Kendall. He was a married man. He had a beautiful wife. But still, he was a very attractive man, with his hazel eyes and his waves of light brown hair and his lanky, athletic body. She was his pupil, that was all, and surely he never thought of *her* improperly. . . .

And then Maude suddenly remembered the day he'd blushed and admitted that he was aware of her femaleness. And then

she remembered yesterday afternoon
when, having finished the lesson of the day
on the use of metaphor in the poems of
Wordsworth, Stephen Kendall closed the
book in front of him, folded his hands behind his head, and suddenly told her, "I
wish you didn't have to go now."

"Me too," she'd said.

"I wish you could stay for the rest of the
afternoon. My manservant would come in
and fix us both a little supper. Nothing
fancy. Some eggs, maybe. Do you like
eggs?"

"Yes," she said. "If they're not runny."

"Me too. A hard-cooked-egg girl, after
my own heart."

They both laughed a little but then both
agreed that they each needed to be elsewhere. Maude was due at choral practice;
she had begun singing in the St. Hilda's
Madrigal Chorus. And Dr. Kendall was due
at home, he said.

"Someday," he told her, "we *will* have
supper. That's a promise. To celebrate your
hard work in the salt mines of the Romantic poets."

"I'll take you up on it," Maude said, and

then she pulled on her brown cloth coat—
and fled.

And now, hearing what Edith had to say,
the entire scene yesterday in Dr. Kendall's
study suddenly had a different quality to it.
It seemed almost . . . well, the best word
was, ironically, *romantic.* There was nothing inappropriate in her tutor's words or his
gestures or his wish that they could have
supper together. But a certain *tenderness*
had been revealed, and thinking about it
now, she realized that it thrilled her.

The next time Maude Latham and
Stephen Kendall met, they studied A. L.
Slayton, working on one of the middle
stanzas of "The Rose and the Stag," and
when they were done, he peered outside at
the late afternoon through the diamond-
shaped panes of glass and asked her
whether she would like to take a walk.

"Yes, fine," said Maude, and she put on
her coat. This was strange but not *that*
strange; tutors were known to share meals
and movies and even cricket matches with
their pupils. Surely a walk together in a
wintry afternoon didn't have much significance. But still Maude became aware of
her increasing heartbeat as they stepped

outside together. The wind was mild, but the temperature was colder than it had seemed from inside the warm study. She was soon shivering without realizing it.

"This won't do," her tutor said as they walked up the High Street. "You're much too cold. Here, take this."

And then he reached up and unwound his scarf from around his neck. It was an oatmeal color, handsomely and elaborately knitted by some careful craftsperson. His wife, perhaps? Maude wondered, picturing Mrs. Kendall sitting in the living room of her gracious Oxford home, two copper knitting needles clicking together rapidly.

"It's beautiful," Maude said, fingering the wool, examining its intricacy of design. "Did . . . Mrs. Kendall knit it for you?"

Much to her surprise, Stephen smiled, as though Maude had told a particularly witty joke. "My wife?" he said. "No, Mrs. Kendall does not 'go in for' knitting." But his smile was dry and joyless.

Maude didn't understand why he was smiling or why there was an ironic edge to his voice. So all she said was, "Oh, I see," even though she didn't see at all.

"My charwoman, Mrs. Laird, made the

scarf for me," he went on. "She's a wonderful woman, and she always sees that I'm warm enough. In fact, my warmth is a central obsession of hers." He turned to Maude and added, "I wish someone was seeing to *your* warmth."

"Oh, I'm all right," said Maude.

"No you're not," Stephen said simply. "I don't think a lifetime of American winters has prepared you for what it's like here."

"Perhaps not," Maude conceded. "But winter is almost over, isn't it?"

"Who knows?" he said. "In England, that's never a given."

There was snow in his hair, a fine silken mist of it; she hadn't even realized it was snowing, yet suddenly she had a foreshadowing of Stephen Kendall as a much older man, distinguished, his hair tinged with a silvery white.

"Listen," he added, "I know I said we ought to go for a walk, and yet it's much too cold now, at least with you in that silly coat of yours. Come, let's duck in here."

They had been standing in front of a tea shop called Trelawny's Savouries and Sweets, and soon they were ensconced at a corner table behind a wide wooden pillar, with plates of currant cake and steaming cups of dark tea in front of them. The air in the room was moist and smelled of wet coats, yet it wasn't unpleasant. There was a warmth and a feeling of enclosure here that Maude found she liked. She and her tutor had both taken off their coats, but she still wore his scarf; she just didn't want to take it off.

"Tell me about yourself," he said as they ate and drank.

"Oh, there's not too much to know," said Maude. "I'm just a fairly typical American girl who decided to go abroad and get a decent education."

"That's the most absurd thing I've ever heard," he said. "Everyone has a *story.* Everyone's life is filled with details. Tell me the story of who you are."

So she began to tell him about growing up in Longwood Falls, and how close she was to her parents, particularly her father. "He gets extremely protective of me," she said. "Especially because of what's happening over here with Germany and Hitler; all the talk about war, all the things you read in the paper. But I always tell him not to worry." Something crossed Dr. Kendall's face quickly, then disappeared. "Do *you* worry?" she asked him then.

He took a moment, then quietly said, "Yes, I do. It seems unlikely that Britain will get into it, and yet, as every day passes and the news gets worse, I just think it's more and more possible that our hand will be forced. And just because we're here in the sheltered community of Oxford doesn't mean we can hide behind our school-books."

"You don't really think—" Maude began, but he cut her off.

"No one knows what to think," he said, his voice slightly curt. "So we can't pretend to try. What I know about are the Romantic poets. Ask me a question about one of them, and I'll tell you everything I can. But when it comes to another country's greed and arrogance and what they're capable of, well, I'm afraid I'm at a loss." He took a long sip of tea, swallowed, then leaned back. "I'm sure I'm being pessimistic," he said in a softer voice. "At least, I hope and pray that I am."

"But if you're not?" asked Maude.

Her tutor shrugged. "Then I'll do what's right. Just like we all will." He closed his eyes, as if shutting out a terrible vision of war, and then he said, "I suppose I should be getting back."

"Mrs. Kendall is waiting?" asked Maude, slightly boldly.

"Mrs. Kendall is waiting," he said with a sigh, and then suddenly he reached out and took Maude's hands in his own. "Oh, Maude," he said, looking straight at her, not blinking. She could barely breathe, she was so shocked. "I just want to say," he went on, "that whenever I know we've got a tutorial that day, it really cheers me up. You see, I've been unhappy for a long time, my wife and I, and—"

"Stop," Maude said. "Please. Dr. Kendall."

"Stephen," he said quickly. "You know my name is Stephen."

"Stephen then," Maude said. "I'm glad I cheer you up. You cheer me up too. But you're my tutor."

He looked away, shaking his head. "God, I wish I wasn't," he said quietly. *Oh, me too,* she thought, *me too,* but she didn't speak. The blood had gone directly to her face; her cheeks were blazing. Unsure of what to do now, Maude took an enormous piece of currant cake and began to eat as though she were starving.

"Maude?" he said. "I've upset you."

"No, no, I'm all right," she replied, but her hand was shaking. Why was it shaking? What was going on here? Nothing made sense to her anymore. She was frightened—not of his feelings for her, but of hers for him. Because what he obviously wanted, she wanted too. Edith had been right: Maude Latham was falling in love with Stephen Kendall. And what was even more astonishing, Stephen Kendall seemed to be falling in love with Maude Latham.

She looked him straight in the eye so that he knew he had not scared her off. She looked and looked; her blue eyes met his hazel eyes, and then both Stephen and Maude began to smile. It was all right; it was better than that. His wife, Mrs. Kendall, whoever she was, simply disappeared in a cloud of pale smoke. It was just Stephen and Maude now; even the clinking of china and the clatter of silver inside Trelawny's had faded away to the barest background noise. They sat at their corner table in the busy tea room behind the wooden pillar and no one was looking at them, no one could see them.

"I feel," said Stephen in a quiet, casual voice, "that if I don't kiss you right now I shall drop dead. I shall simply fall forward onto the table and that will be that."

"Oh," said Maude in a whisper, and then she couldn't say another word. He moved toward her and she toward him; his mouth was hot from the tea, the lips extremely soft. He tasted of currant cake and the smoky essence of the tea. She was eighteen years old and had never kissed any man like this before, a long, impossibly wonderful kiss, and by the time it was over she understood that her dream of "knowing the world" was about to be realized.

Over the following weekend, Maude kept to herself, not wanting to talk to anyone about what had happened, but just wanting to savor it, to turn it over and over in her mind. She went by herself into town on Saturday wearing Stephen's scarf, which she'd forgotten to give back to him. She'd return it on Tuesday afternoon at their tutorial; until then, feeling the thick wool around her throat somehow made her feel safe, as though she were with him, as though he were holding her. For now, she walked into town and stepped into the covered market to buy a present for Edith, whose birthday was coming up. There among all the various cramped shops selling meat and fabric and books and watches, Maude bought a box of sugared orange peel, for Edith loved anything sweet. It was when she was on her way out of the little shop that she saw him. Her arm immediately shot up in order to wave to him and call him over.

And then she realized that he was with his wife.

There she was, the woman from the photograph on his desk, as beautiful in life as she was inside that silver frame, a cool, fashionable woman in a fur coat and a hat that had a long feather sweeping up from the side. Her complexion was unlined, her eyes heavy-lidded and perhaps bored. She was taller than he was, and carried herself regally. Stephen walked along beside her with his hands thrust into his coat pockets. Both of them looked miserable. They didn't touch, they didn't talk to each other. They looked like a couple you might see on a street and about whom you might think: Their marriage is in deep trouble.

Maude lowered her arm slowly. Should she run away, pretend she hadn't seen him? She realized that there was no protocol for this; she'd never remotely been in a similar position before. He was her tutor. They'd kissed each other once; maybe it had been one of those spontaneous, spur-of-the-moment occurrences that would never be repeated, never be spoken of again.

He saw her now, and he too seemed to be deciding what to do. There was a split second of indecision, and then he raised his own arm and called out, "Miss Latham?"

Maude looked at him and smiled, pretending to be surprised. "Dr. Kendall," she said, and then he came over to her and introduced her to his wife.

"Helena, this is one of my finer pupils," he said. "Maude Latham, all the way from the U.S. of A."

Helena Kendall was sizing her up, discreetly regarding her the way one woman regards another in the presence of a male who is of mutual interest.

"Hello," Stephen's wife said. "Good to meet you."

She held out a gloved hand, and Maude took it; the hand was small and seemed somehow clawlike in its gray suede glove with the single mother-of-pearl button at the wrist. "Good to meet you too," Maude said. And then, before her eyes, Helena Kendall's slightly threatened expression changed, turning into something darker. Hatred, perhaps? She was staring at Maude strangely, and that was when Maude realized what it was: *Stephen's scarf.*

"Oh," she said quickly. "I see you're looking at the scarf." Then, trying to appear casual, she unwound it from her neck. "Your husband was kind enough to lend it to me the other day when I was leaving his study, because I'm afraid I had no idea how cold England gets." Maude thrust the scarf in Stephen's arms, then turned to him. "Sorry I forgot to return it," she said. "Here you go."

"Yes, right, my scarf," Stephen said vaguely.

During this exchange Helena Kendall's face relaxed a bit, returning to its previous expression. And yet Maude understood that she'd made a mistake wearing the scarf out today; she'd aroused Stephen's wife's suspicions. It had been a stupid thing to do, and yet she had no way of undoing it. "Next time," Maude said in what she hoped was a cheerful, jaunty voice, "maybe you'll lend me earmuffs."

Then, before she could get herself into any more trouble, Maude turned and skittered off, hurrying out of the covered market and back into the frozen afternoon, her neck now exposed to the icy wind.

When she saw him on Tuesday, he wasn't the least bit angry. "It was just one of those things," he said. "Don't fret about it. When I saw you in the market, my heart was leaping. I swear, Maude, I could almost have turned to Helena and said 'There's the girl I kissed!' "

"I'm glad you didn't," Maude said.

"Me too. She'd have my head on a platter. The thing about Helena is that, even though she doesn't love me or kiss me or even speak civilly to me, she actually wants to continue being my wife. I don't really understand it, but it's the way it is. We've got nothing left to say to each other, and yet she enjoys the *idea* of being married to me, although our marriage itself is a dismal disaster."

"Was it always that way?" Maude asked tentatively.

"Oh no," said Stephen. "Once it was different, but everything changed soon after the wedding. She's a fragile woman emotionally, and I knew that when we got married, but I told myself it wouldn't matter. In fact, it did." He took a breath. "She gets these moods. They come and go. She'll suddenly take to her bed and stay there for weeks. And at other times she becomes very angry and jealous, accusing me of being unfaithful, of being a liar, of being a terrible person." He paused again. "We have no relationship, none at all, but she's so delicate that I haven't brought up the subject of ending our marriage. There hasn't really been a need for that. Until now."

Maude was quiet, taking in his words. Then she said, "About the scarf. Do you think she knows?"

At that moment Stephen stood up from his chair and walked behind Maude's chair. He leaned over her, kissing her hair, the nape of her neck. "There's nothing to know yet, really," he said softly. "Although I'd like there to be."

"What are you saying?" she asked, but she knew.

"I want to make love to you," said Stephen. "I want it more than anything I can remember wanting."

Maude tipped her head down, glanced at her hands in her lap. She didn't know what to say; she'd never had a moment like this in her life.

"I'm sorry," Stephen said quickly. "That was too much. Too soon for you."

"No, no," Maude replied. "It wasn't. What you want . . . I think I want it too."

"I'm so glad," said Stephen.

They stayed there like that a little longer, she in the oversize chair, he standing right behind her, leaning down almost protectively, hovering like a good angel, and all thoughts of poetry seemed suddenly as far away as a land on the other side of an ocean.

CHAPTER THREE

When Maude was a child, her parents would take her on the train down to New York City twice a year. It was always her idea. There was never anything in particular that she wanted to do, nothing special she had been begging them to see. She didn't ask to go to the Easter pageant at Radio City Music Hall, didn't dream about Broadway or the ballet, though her parents always wound up taking her to all those places, and more. For Maude Latham it was enough simply to be in the City. She understood that Manhattan was just an island, that some of the streets that ran between river and river were shorter than Main Street in Longwood Falls. But they *seemed* to stretch forever. If you were a five- or seven- or ten-year-old girl, you couldn't actually see where they ended, through all the buildings and traffic and crowds, and so you could imagine that they went on forever. That no matter how far you followed them, you could always go farther. That no matter how many corners you turned, you would always find one more. One of Maude's earliest memories was of her first trip down to New York, of glancing out the window of the train and seeing the skyline. That morning Maude thought Manhattan really was a castle out of a fairy tale, or a kingdom of some sort, and in a way that's what it always remained in her imagination: endless corridors and canyons, halls and stages, spires and turrets and secret passages, a place to lose yourself exploring. But now, on the train from Oxford to London, Maude understood that cities also offered a more adult possibility: a place to lose yourself, period.

She and Stephen were sitting side by side in a compartment across from two other passengers, a dozing elderly woman who clutched an ugly alligator handbag against herself, and a man in a brown suit reading the *Financial Times*. The four pas-

sengers had nodded their hellos at the beginning of the trip, briefly acknowledging
one another's presence before retreating
into themselves. Then the train began to
rock evenly, the woman's eyes closed, and
the man unfolded his newspaper. That was
all there was to it.

After an hour the train would pull into
Waterloo Station and the woman would
awaken and the man would lower his
newspaper, and the four of them would
leave the compartment and join the other
passengers from all the other compart-
ments crowding onto the platform to
stream out of the station into the streets
and go their separate ways, and the elderly
woman and the well-dressed man would
never see Stephen and Maude again,
would never even *think* of them again, and
that was as it should be. That was why
Stephen and Maude were going to London.

"I know the perfect place there,"
Stephen had said to Maude after their
most recent tutorial as he walked her back
to her residence.

"It sounds wonderful," Maude said.

"But I haven't told you a thing about it,"

said Stephen. "I haven't even told you its name."

"It doesn't matter," she said. "If you think it's perfect, then I'm sure it is."

They were walking side by side, together but not "together." Not touching. Not daring even to look each other in the eye. "Together" was something they couldn't afford to be seen to be, not in Oxford, anyway. The encounter in the covered marketplace with Stephen's wife had vividly demonstrated the dangers of letting their guard down, even for a moment. Anyone seeing them now, noting how they spoke tersely and nodded agreement as they passed beneath a row of marble arches, might have thought they were simply a tutor and a student deep in a philosophical discussion.

Which, in a way, they were. They had agreed in Stephen's study that this was not the place to follow such an impetuous and risky course of action. Not in Stephen's study, certainly, but not in Oxford at all. Where was the romance in a hurried clinch in which they'd have to keep one ear out for the knock of a manservant, the return of a suite mate? Where was the romance in *anything* hurried, any shadowy liaison in a residence hall or local inn where half their attention would be elsewhere, where their devotion to each other would by necessity be less than complete?

And romance was what they wanted: the Romantic vision that had brought them together, the complete devotion immortalized in the soaring words of poets who had dared to live their lives to the fullest, who had stopped at nothing in the pursuit of beauty and love. And it was romance that Stephen and Maude would have. Just not in Oxford.

"In London, then," Stephen said that afternoon in his study.

"Yes," Maude answered.

"This weekend," Stephen said.

He was standing behind Maude's chair. She couldn't see him, but she could hear him. And not just his voice; also his breath, which was coming in short, sharp bursts. And then she noticed her own rapid-fire breathing, the birdcage beating of her heart. Stephen was right; something important was happening between them, something that deserved more than whatever they could manage here, under circumstances that would have had to be less than ideal.

And so they gathered themselves up in Stephen's study, straightening their slightly rumpled clothes, smoothing their hair. But still they couldn't bear to be apart, not yet, and so Stephen had offered to walk Maude back to her rooms, and she had accepted, and then they had crossed the quadrangles between Stephen's study and the entrance to St. Hilda's proper, hoping that they appeared to be anything but what they were: a man and woman who were falling in love, two almost-lovers plotting how to steal away by themselves.

"Now, I can't vouch for this place I have in mind, you understand," Stephen said.

"It doesn't matter."

"I know it only by name. Really, I've just heard of it, and that's all."

"Stephen, I don't care."

"I know, I know," he said. "It's just that I want everything to be—"

"Perfect."

He laughed. "I must sound like a perfect idiot."

"No," Maude said. "You sound like a perfect *Romantic.*"

They stopped. They had reached the tall wrought-iron gates with their twisting brass vines. For the first time since leaving Stephen's study, they turned to face each other fully. Their breath hung in the cold air, clouding the space between them.

"Our restraint is admirable, wouldn't you say?" Stephen said.

"Ah, is that the word for it, *admirable*?" asked Maude. "I'll have to remember that. I didn't know restraint was such a virtue among the Romantics."

Stephen smiled his familiar shy smile. A crowd of girls were passing by, one laugh rising above the others.

"Saturday, then," Stephen said, in a formal voice, for the benefit of anyone who might be overhearing their conversation.

"Yes, Saturday, Dr. Kendall," Maude said, hesitating slightly on the sidewalk, in the chill evening air, before hurrying to follow the female students inside.

And now, finally, Saturday had come. Maude had thought of little else since last seeing Stephen. She had told Edith and the officials who gave clearance for students to briefly leave the university that she would be going down to London for the weekend to visit an uncle from the States who was in Europe on a diplomatic mission. Maude was surprised at how easily the lie came to her, and how readily even suspicious, sophisticated Edith had accepted it. Stephen had lied to his wife too, telling her he needed to do some research in London for a paper he was writing.

But the lying, she hoped, was over for now—the lying and evasions and pavement pantomimes and awkward encounters in market stalls. At least for one weekend, Maude wanted to be herself, and Stephen to be himself, and nobody to be any the wiser. Sinking back in her seat on the train, still keeping a discreet separation between herself and Stephen, Maude asked herself, just as she'd asked again and again over the previous twenty-four and forty-eight and seventy-two hours since she'd last seen Stephen: Is this how she'd always imagined it would be—falling in love?

No.

No: But only because she had *not* imagined it. Not really. Not like this. Not before Stephen, anyway.

Maude had noticed boys in high school, of course. She couldn't *not* notice them, the way their shoulders broadened over the course of a summer, their chins roughened. But then what? What came after the kiss and the prom and the promise to write each other regularly from college? That was where Maude's imagination always failed her. No, that wasn't quite true; that's where the imagination of the boys she knew back home failed *them.* Because what could they offer a girl who wanted . . . well, who wanted more than whatever it was they could offer *her*?

The more likely scenario all along, she supposed, had been something like the one she was living now. If she'd been asked a year or so ago, she might have said that yes, knowing herself the way she did and knowing what she wanted out of life, she could see herself meeting a man one day in some far-off city and spending the rest of her life with him. And once she'd been accepted to Oxford she might have even imagined that city would be London. But the possibility of romance was not what had enticed her overseas in an uncertain, even perilous time.

What she felt with Stephen was something she'd never imagined for herself, because she hadn't *known* to imagine it. Because how could you imagine *this*? Who, in advance, could possibly be equipped to imagine what the mere presence of another person could do to your very being?

Who knew?

Nobody, Maude suspected. Never. Not one single soul—until it happened to you.

And even then you *still* didn't know. That was the frightening part. It was easy to sip sherry and read poetry and experience that gentle, warm, wavelike surge that made you close your eyes and place your hand over your heart. And it was even easier when the person you were reading poetry with was Stephen Kendall. But what did it mean to be unable to imagine anyone who could ever make you happier than this person? Did that say something more about you than it did about him? Was it simply a failure of imagination on your part—a schoolgirl crush, the kind of thing everyone else at Longwood Falls High had felt a couple of years ago, one more stage for you to outgrow? Or was this really something else—the kind of love that poets had written about since the beginning of time?

There was only one way to find out, and Maude was taking it. Sitting in a compartment of a train across from a woman with her eyes closed and a man whose face was obscured by a newspaper, Maude reached out, and Stephen allowed his hand to be taken in hers.

Stephen reached out, and Maude allowed her arm to be taken in his. They were walking up a road just outside Waterloo Station. The sidewalk was crowded with flower peddlers and passengers from the Oxford train ducking into blocky black taxis or scattering down an entrance to the Underground, and newspaper broadsheets covered in the same big grim letters that they always seemed to be carrying these days. Hitler's name was everywhere, terrifying, depressing, impossible to avoid. A light rain had begun to fall, and Stephen had quickly raised a black umbrella—or "brolly," as he called it. But even if he hadn't, and even if the sidewalk were as clear as a cloudless sky, Stephen and Maude still might have leaned into each other fully now, availing themselves of the freedom afforded them simply by the fact of being in London.

"Oh, Stephen, look."

Maude said this almost before she realized it—almost before she realized what it was she'd read that prompted her to say it. For the words she'd seen up ahead were so familiar to her that she barely needed to read them to recognize them. But there they were, above the sidewalk up the street, to her amazement hanging on a sign: THE ROSE AND STAG.

"Stephen, do you see?"

"Oh, my darling Maude," he said.

Maude turned toward him. "You've heard of it?" she said.

He began to laugh lightly, then said, "I told you I knew the perfect place in London."

It didn't take poetry, she knew then. She'd drunk no sherry, read no verse, but what she felt at that moment needed nothing magical to manufacture it.

"Now remember, I can't personally vouch for it," Stephen said. "But I recalled vaguely from my research that there was this place in London that A. L. Slayton used to frequent back when he was a young moody writer. It had some typical name: The Brigadier, or the King's Guard, something unmemorable. After he died so young, poor man, the owners changed the name to honor his memory. The pub downstairs"—he added casually—"and the inn above."

They continued walking in the rain in silence, sheltered under the awning of the umbrella. When they reached the entrance to the inn, Stephen pulled open a large wooden door, and he and Maude ducked into a dim lobby that was dark and small but not untidy.

"Well," said Stephen when he'd finished struggling to close the umbrella and had a chance to look around, "it seems as if it hasn't changed much since old Slayton stayed here."

"I love it," Maude said.

Stephen smiled down at Maude and then something came over his face.

"You really are so beautiful," he said softly. "I know it's only been a matter of days now, but I feel as if we've waited forever for this moment."

"So do I," she said.

He lowered his face to hers, and Maude closed her eyes.

A slight noise then, the scraping of a chair, caught their attention. Maude turned quickly to find a counter that she hadn't noticed earlier, off to one side of the lobby, and a terribly thin old man behind it pushing himself to his feet.

She took a step back. Stephen cleared his throat and approached the counter.

"Hello, sir," he said. "I've booked a room."

"It's a bit early in the day," the man said. "I'm afraid we've nothing quite ready at the moment. Mr. and Mrs.—?"

"Wick," Stephen said, and Maude shot him a look of surprise.

"I've only the wife working upstairs now," the old man went on. "Had to let the other girl go. Not so many people coming to London to see the sights these days, don't you know. Fact is, you'll pretty much have the place to yourself tonight, if you don't mind. Not London, I mean. The inn upstairs. Still, you might soon say the same of London. I suppose you've heard the latest."

"The latest?" Stephen said.

"P.M. says if Germany invades Poland, we're in it. Us and the French. Ah, here we are," the man said, landing his long finger on a line in the reservation ledger. "Mr. and Mrs. Wick. Check-in time's not till three, but I expect your room will be ready before then. You can leave your bags here, if you like. Go out and see the sights while there's still sights to see, I like to say these days."

"Actually," said Stephen, "I expect we'll just be waiting in the pub."

The man looked up at them now as if for the first time. He removed his rimless spectacles and seemed to consider them anew. Maude looped her arm through Stephen's.

"Newlyweds, are you?" the old man said, replacing his spectacles.

"You could say that," Stephen said.

"I can always tell. Talent of mine. Wife always says to mind me own business, but I know these things, I do." He slammed the register shut. "Well, we'll fix you up with a right proper room."

"Thanks so much," Stephen said. "Actually, I was wondering." He stopped, and the man looked at him over the tops of his spectacles. "It's an odd request, but you wouldn't happen to know which room it was that A. L. Slayton used to stay in? I understand that after an evening of drinking he sometimes retired upstairs."

The man shook his head. "Don't know any Slayton," he said. "Can you describe the fellow?"

"Ah," Stephen said. "Never mind. We'll just be in the pub, then."

Stephen and Maude were barely able to contain their laughter long enough to cross the lobby of the inn and enter the pub. Once inside, though, they quickly regained their composure.

They'd arrived at the end of the lunchtime rush. A barmaid balancing a tray on one high hand barely had enough room to maneuver between the men lining the bar in the center of the room and the tables along the window. Even so, despite the crowd, Maude couldn't help noticing that the noise level was unnaturally low. Somber, almost. The two barmen in white aprons pulling beer from the long golden spigots were going about their task with identical cheerless blank expressions, as if dispensing medicine. The clinking of cutlery easily overwhelmed the conversations, which seemed to be taking place at a great distance, or underwater. Here and there a word escaped, rising to the surface: *Poland. France. Germany.*

Stephen gripped Maude by the shoulders and steered her toward an open table near the window. Then, while he went to the bar to place their order, Maude sat straight in her wooden chair and stared outside.

The rain had stopped. The street shone blackly, and Maude found that if she pressed her forehead against the small pane of glass and looked up, she could just make out a slice of blue. Seeing that sky, she thought, it was possible, with sufficient effort, to imagine that life as anyone in this pub knew it might yet return to normal.

"Wick, indeed," Maude said, when Stephen returned with their two pints of ale. "I almost burst out laughing."

He allowed himself a thin smile. "Yes, I thought you might enjoy that little nod to the late and apparently unlamented A. L. Slayton," he said, settling onto his wooden stool. " 'Her small hand reach'd out to waken the *wick* with flame,' " he quoted from the poem, " 'And he saw her eyes were wild . . .' "

"Well, here's to A. L. Slayton, then," Maude said, raising her glass.

"Yes." Stephen raised his glass too. But then his expression wavered, clouded over for a moment, and instead of drinking he placed the glass back on the tabletop. "Maude," he said, "I have to say, I can't believe you're here."

"In London, you mean?" she said, placing her own pint glass back carefully on the table, balancing it between both hands, as if the moment somehow required some extra measure of delicacy. "With you?"

Stephen smiled uncertainly and looked down at his drink. "Well, yes. That too," he said. "But I meant *here.*" He looked up. "England. Now, of all times."

Maude looked away. "We've had this conversation," she said softly.

"Not really," he said. "Every time I've brought it up, you've changed the subject."

"Oh, Stephen, please don't do this." She shook her head.

"I know," he said. "But I worry." Stephen leaned forward. "Look, let's be realistic here—"

"Why?" Maude said, and the sharpness in her voice surprised her. "Why should I? Why should I start being realistic now? If I were *realistic,* I wouldn't be here at all. And I don't mean here in England, now, with who-knows-what waiting to break loose right across the Channel. I mean *here,* in London, with you, at this table in the Rose and Stag. Don't you understand, darling? Realistic girls don't leave a loving home in a small town. Realistic girls don't go off on their own across the ocean to Oxford. Realistic girls," she said bitterly, "don't fall in love with a married man."

She stopped. She'd said more than she meant to say, more than she even knew she'd wanted to say. Maude raised one hand to her mouth.

"Well," Stephen said, after a long moment, lifting his pint glass. "To unrealistic girls, then."

Maude couldn't help but laugh, mostly with relief that she hadn't upset him. "Stephen, do you really think I don't know the danger?" she asked. "Do you honestly believe I don't understand that I'd be safer somewhere far away from here?"

"I want you to promise me," he said. "Promise me that if things really heat up, you'll go back to the States."

"But I can't do that," she said. "I can't make that promise. I have to see this through—whatever it is that's happening between us. Who would I be if I didn't? I certainly wouldn't be the kind of girl who would interest you. Was Keats realistic? Shelley? Slayton?"

"But you forget, darling. They all died young."

"I'm prepared to do that," said Maude, without thinking about what she was saying.

Stephen pushed back from the table. "Oh, now you really are talking nonsense."

"Am I? Who was it who said that when it comes to stopping Hitler, he'd gladly enlist?"

"I was talking about dying for my country. I don't think anyone should be dying for *me* personally."

"Well, that's not your decision to make, Stephen. And," she added, staring at him long enough until he looked her back in the eye, "I can't honestly believe you wouldn't make the same choice if our positions were reversed."

Stephen looked down. He began playing with his beer, tracing circles around the lip of the glass with his fingertip. "You mean that, don't you?" he said without looking up.

"Are you surprised?" Maude said.

"No. No, I'm not surprised. Not at all. Because you're right, of course. That's the absolute hell of it. What you're saying makes sense." His voice was softer now. "We do have choices to make. Each of us."

"But not now," Maude added. "Not this weekend. Please. Promise me. No more talk about 'being realistic.' "

She reached across the table, opening both hands. Stephen took them in his own.

"No, not this weekend," he agreed. "I'm sorry. You're quite right, as usual. No more talk of anything unpleasant. Now, then. Shall we see if our room is ready?"

The room, on the top floor of the inn, was simple but sweet. On one side was a dormer window that looked out over the same road leading to Waterloo Station that

Stephen and Maude had walked up that morning. Through the partly open window came a light breeze that lifted and bowed the sheer curtains, filling the room with the first hint of spring. On the other side of the room was a dresser, on top of which sat a blue porcelain pitcher and bowl. The walls were bare, but their yellow hue was nonetheless warm. Someone had done what they could with what they had. The one extravagance waited in the center of the room, in the middle of the bedspread with its pattern of little grapes on vines: a single rose.

"A gift for the honeymoon couple, I take it," Stephen said.

"It's perfect," Maude said. "It really is. Everything about this place."

"Well, that *is* all I wanted, if you recall," Stephen said. "Perfection. That's not too much to ask, now, is it? But if that's the rose," he went on, turning from the bed, "where is the stag, I wonder?"

"Right here," Maude said, moving into his arms and patting one hand flat against Stephen's chest.

"Which would make you," he said, "my rose. I believe you still owe me a kiss from the lobby of this establishment, Mrs. Wick."

Maude tilted her face. The same expression came over Stephen's face then that she'd seen in the lobby hours earlier, a look of longing and expectation and relief. It was a look, Maude realized, she wished would never disappear.

"No," she said.

"What?" said Stephen.

"Not yet. Just let me look at you."

"Look at me?"

"Yes. Just . . . look at you."

"All right."

"I know it's odd," she said. "But I don't want this moment to pass. I want to hold it here for as long as I can. Hold *you* here for as long as I can. Do you understand?" He nodded, not speaking. "That wouldn't be a bad way to spend a lifetime, would it?"

"No," he whispered. "No, not at all. I like the idea, actually. You know," he added, "I think you've got a touch of the poet yourself."

"Maybe it's this room. Or the inn. Or the ghost of A. L. Slayton."

"Maybe it's you," Stephen said.

"No," Maude said. "I know what it is. It's

you. It's being with you. That's all it is."
Then she said, "Yes."

"Yes," Stephen echoed. "Yes."

And then he lowered his face to hers.

She took in a sharp breath; it wasn't as
though she wasn't prepared for this moment, or wasn't ready. She was. But still,
because it was her first time and her feelings were so strong, she was almost overwhelmed by the sensations that caused
her to close her eyes and moan softly and
reach out to touch him everywhere, to feel
his warm skin against her, to run her hands
through the soft thicket of hair on his
chest, and along the musculature of his
shoulders. And she wanted him to touch
her everywhere too—to become ac-
quainted with her entire body as though it
was itself a *person,* separate from her. Her
need was unrelenting; it surprised her. She
realized that somehow she *longed* for
Stephen even in the moments when he
was indisputably hers.

That night, Maude awoke at some unde-
termined hour. A siren was summoning her.
Where was this?

No, not her. Not summoning her. Someone. A siren, shrilling in the street.

London, she remembered. *Stephen.*

London. A siren. Summoning everyone: out. Out now. Get out now!

Maude turned quickly under the quilt, now fully awake.

The room was dark. Stephen was there, lying next to her, breathing evenly. And the siren, she could hear now, was only a siren, just another noise in a city at night. Some unfortunate soul heading to hospital, nothing more.

She thought of the man on the train yesterday morning, reading the newspaper. The sleeping woman clutching her handbag to her bosom.

The insistent cry of the siren faded. Maude pulled her nightgown from the bedpost and wrapped herself in it as she crossed to the dormer window. She sat on the white wooden ledge there and looked out. The street was empty now, abandoned. She thought of the flower peddler they'd passed yesterday morning—probably the woman from whom the proprietor of the inn had bought the rose to lay on the bed. Everyone was gone now, safely home, inside, lights out, dreaming. The blue sky she'd studied through the window in the pub that afternoon: gone too.

The world turned; night fell; a weekend came and went. You could stare into the eyes of a lover and touch him and make love to him only so long.

"Maude?"

It was Stephen, calling softly to her in the dark. Maude turned toward the bed. She could see in the faint light from the window that he'd propped himself up on one elbow.

"I'm sorry," she said. "Something woke me."

"Me too," he said. "Your absence."

Maude crossed the wooden floor back to the bed. She sat on the edge and reached out toward Stephen's sleepy, blurry face. He turned at her touch, aroused, closing his eyes and kissing her palm.

"Where do you want to go in the morning?" he asked groggily. "You're in London. One of the great cities of the world." He opened his eyes then and said, "Oh, darling, you're crying."

"I'm sorry," she said. "I don't mean to.

I've just been thinking, that's all. There was a siren; it woke me up. I don't want to leave here."

He sat up now suddenly, folding his arms around her and holding her tightly. She sagged against his chest, let herself cry.

"We'll come back here," Stephen said. "Soon. I promise. We'll come up with all kinds of excuses that will allow us to get away."

"I know, I know. It's not that. It's—I'm sorry. I tried. Really I did."

"Tried what? I don't understand."

"Here I was the one in the pub begging you not to be 'realistic' just for this one weekend, and here I am waking you up with my worries in the middle of the night."

"I don't mind," he said. "I rather like it."

She brushed both her cheeks with the back of a hand, composing herself as best she could. "So. All right then. Where shall we go tomorrow?"

"Maude."

"I have a funny way with cities," she said. "You should know that about me. When I was a little girl I would go with my parents into New York City—"

"Maude," he said again.

She stopped talking.

"It's all right to be scared," he said.

"I know." She turned away, swiveled her body on the bed. It was then that she saw the rose. It was on the nightstand in a glass of water, right where they'd left it the previous afternoon. Even in the dark in the middle of the night, its bloom was unmistakably present.

"It's just that I don't want to lose you," she said.

"You won't."

"You don't know that," Maude said. "You can't make that promise."

Stephen was quiet for several moments before he answered.

"No," he said. "If there's a war, you're quite right. I can't."

She turned toward him.

"There," Stephen said. "That's my concession to realism for the weekend. My only concession, mind you."

Maude smiled. "Thank you," she said. "Now tell me about the morning. And the afternoon too. Where we'll go before we have to return to Oxford."

Stephen fell back against his pillow then,

hands folded behind his head. "Well, yes. All right then. First," he said, "I suggest that we walk everywhere and go nowhere."

"Sounds perfect."

She rested her head against his chest. They lay there for a long time then, in the fragile silence, in the darkness, Stephen simply breathing until his breaths had regained the deep and even rhythm of sleep, and Maude, lying awake, simply listening to the beat of his heart.

CHAPTER FOUR

Though she had only been alive for nineteen years, Maude Latham knew that what she had found with Stephen was the genuine article. She knew it right away after that first day at the Rose and Stag, and she continued to believe it as the academic year passed by in a flurry. Remarkably, their love affair didn't keep her from being an excellent student; being with him was so intense, so undiluted, that she needed a respite from time to time, and immersing herself in Latin or history or botany provided just that. It was only when she studied Romantic poetry that Maude felt herself dropping deeper into her reverie, for Stephen was of course the person she studied it with, and the words of the poems themselves were relevant to their situation right now.

Particularly A. L. Slayton, who was both Stephen's and Maude's favorite. "The Rose and the Stag"—the poem—and the Rose and Stag—the inn—had become central in their lives. Throughout that spring and the entire summer of 1939, Maude and Stephen invented excuses to go down to London in order to spend several hours together, if not an entire night, at the Rose and Stag. And even when they couldn't, they stole an hour or two in his study, or at a remote area along the Thames where the only people they ever tended to see were fishermen. Maude had decided to stay on in Oxford during the summer months, having arranged to work as a research assistant for her botany tutor. The university and the city too had emptied out considerably, due not only to the end of the term but also to the increased fears about Hitler's next moves. Maude spent her mornings studying poetry with Stephen, lying against him, their heads tilted as they read aloud to each other. Sometimes they spoke of what it would be like when they were married, when they didn't have to see each other in secret, when they could be together all the time.

"We'll have a family," he said once, then hastily added, "if you'd like that."

"Yes," she said. "I would."

"Good," he said, and then he told her that Helena hadn't wanted children, that she'd felt she wasn't up to it, disposition-wise, and it was clear from his tone that this was a source of sadness for him. This and many other facts of his life with Helena.

He was very unhappily married; his marriage was a farce, he said, in which neither partner had anything to say to the other anymore, and yet he had to act cautiously; he had to speak to Helena about a divorce only when she seemed strong enough to cope, and when she would not fly into a punitive rage about losing him. That moment hadn't come yet, but he swore it would one day very soon. Maude would wait. She was absorbed in her work, and in following the news about Germany in the papers and on the radio each day. Stephen had taught her to play croquet, at which she proved to be positively mediocre. She spent her afternoons in Dr. Lyman's laboratory, peering at leaves and thistles under a microscope and dutifully making notations in a journal, then dating and bagging the specimens. The job barely paid at all but just allowed her to stay in her rooms and take meals at St. Hilda's, where she would continue to live in the fall when classes re-sumed—assuming Britain didn't go to war. But it would have been foolish to assume any such thing, Maude knew.

As the summer progressed, though, along with her deepening relationship with Stephen and their discussions of marriage, an even greater fear about war insinuated itself into the Oxford community. Posters were slapped up on signposts advertising emergency information sessions and meet-ings where government officials would be available for answering questions. And then, in August, Hitler fatefully joined forces with Joseph Stalin, prompting Maude's fa-ther to send a letter:

My dear Maudie,
It saddens your mother and me no end that you are being so obstinate! You can plainly see for yourself that you are living in a very unstable place. I told you as early as last October, when Hitler took over the Sudetenland, that I

felt you were too close to the action for comfort (mine, apparently, not yours). But you insisted that you would be fine, and so far you have been correct. But that is no longer true. With the deadly and frankly terrifying alliance of Herr Hitler and Mr. Stalin, I fear and pray for your country and all the other ones nearby. As a U.S. citizen I am concerned about Europe—gravely concerned. But as a father, I am concerned about YOU, and so you can't miss the fact that I've enclosed with this letter a one-way ticket from Southampton to New York Harbor, once again aboard the *Queen Mary.* You have always been a clever girl, never a fool. PLEASE DON'T BECOME ONE NOW. Your mother and I and Ruthie and James all love you far too much to let you endanger yourself like this. Your education and need for adventure can wait, darling; you can go back to Oxford when all of this nonsense is over.

Your loving father

Maude let the letter drop into her lap like a floating leaf. She knew he was right, of course, but what kept her here in England was not some misguided sense of safety or misguided need for adventure or an Oxford education, but simply the depth of her attachment to Stephen. He was her lover, her whole life now, the man she was going to marry as soon as he was free, but of course she couldn't tell her father such a thing. Stephen too wanted her to leave England, telling her that even if she went back to the States now, they would be together as husband and wife soon enough, if only she would be patient. But she couldn't be away from him. If he stayed, so would she.

And so Maude found herself sitting in her rooms in St. Hilda's on the first day of September in 1939 when someone came running frantically along the corridor shouting something unintelligible. Maude swung open her door; there stood Leslie Bakemore, a mathematics student with bright red hair. Her face was fiery now too as she cried to Maude, all in a rush, "Hitler's invaded Poland, and Jesus Christ, you know what that means!"

Two days later, Britain and France had declared war on Germany, and much of

Oxford was hysterically packing. Steamer trunks were pushed through doors, the clothes still poking through the sides. The War Office established itself in various buildings of the different colleges; Keble College was suddenly filled with secretaries and cipher clerks, and the Ministry of Food had commandeered St. John's. School was nominally still in session, but the war had trumped everything, giving the university a grim new role, reminding all the faculty and staff who had been there for a long time of World War I, the so-called Great War, which had stolen so many young and promising lives from within these same walls.

Stephen was nowhere to be found; he wasn't in his study or in the library, and of course Maude couldn't call him at home; she'd never been able to do that. She knew that she had to face what was coming; it roiled her stomach and made her dizzy to even think about it, but of course he'd been preparing her for it all year. With the war a reality, Stephen was going to join the British forces, and it was only a matter of time before she heard it for herself.

Late that night when Maude was pacing

her rooms anxiously, a spray of pebbles struck one of her windows. She ran to look out and saw Stephen in the courtyard below; he'd never dared to approach her at her college residence before. Stephen wasn't smiling. He was standing there under the moon with his head lifted toward her, just waiting. In his arms he held something wrapped in brown paper. She hurried downstairs, babbled some excuse to the matron at the front desk, and then rushed out into the courtyard.

"Quickly," he said. "Let's go over here."

He led her to a columned walkway; mossy busts of figures in Oxford history loomed silently all around them. But there was no innocent leisure to the gesture; he wasn't a boy in love waiting to meet his girl in order to steal a few kisses. He wasn't Romeo climbing a tree to find Juliet on the balcony. He was a grown man, weary-looking, troubled, and when he spoke to her his voice was grave.

"We knew this might happen," Stephen reminded her. "So I want you to listen to me, Maude. I'm leaving tomorrow, joining the Royal Navy. I've been planning it for some time, and it's all been worked out."

"But where will you be stationed?" she asked.

"I don't know," said Stephen, shaking his head. "But the thing is, even when I do know, I can't tell you. I won't be able to be in touch for security reasons. That's the way it is and the way it has to be. Any correspondence could be intercepted by the other side, and my location could be compromised."

"I know," said Maude, but she was crying now, the tears streaming down her face and into her mouth, even though she'd tried so hard to remain collected. In wartime, love didn't matter; in wartime, love became irrelevant. Maude quickly realized this and tried as hard as she could to keep her anguish to herself, because it felt selfish. Stephen was going away; he would be putting on his Royal Navy uniform, and leaving for parts unknown. He was going to fight the Germans, and it was possible he would never return.

But she couldn't entertain this possibility, not really. He had to return; he couldn't be in danger. Stephen held her, pressing her against him and whispering into her hair, but it did no good.

"You *will* go back home to the States, of course," Stephen said, though in the past she'd told him she wouldn't. "The government is ordering that all women and children be evacuated to the countryside."

It wasn't a question, it was a statement: Of course she would go back home. And yet Maude treated it as a question, for she quickly answered, "No."

"No?" said Stephen. "What do you mean? You're going to go to the countryside instead?"

Maude shook her head. "I live here now," she said, "and I want to be useful. I'm going to go to London and work for the war effort." The idea was forming while she spoke. "Surely they can't send *all* the women away; surely they'll need nurses," she continued.

"But you're not a nurse," Stephen said.

"I can become one," she said simply.

"You're crazy," he said, but she heard a hint of admiration in his voice.

England had become her adopted country; Maude felt completely at home here. And she wanted to do something useful, as he was doing, and she wanted to stay here near where he would be.

"You can't just walk into some hospital and say 'Hello, I'm a literature student at Oxford who'd like to be a nurse,' " Stephen told her.

"I don't believe you," said Maude. "If I tell them I want to learn, how can they turn me away? The Royal Navy didn't turn you away."

"No," he said. "That's true." They were quiet for a moment. He pulled back then and looked at her. "It's dark now, and it's hard to see," Stephen said, "but I want to remember your face."

"Don't say that," said Maude. "It sounds so final."

"But I have to," he insisted. "If anything happens to me—"

"Nothing's going to happen."

"It might," said Stephen gently. "And I want to think about the girl from St. Hilda's College, Oxford—"

"Oh, please don't do this," interrupted Maude.

"—the extremely intelligent and beautiful literature student who loves the poems of A. L. Slayton as much as I do, and who will always be my girl, no matter what happens, who will always be my rose—"

"Please stop," Maude said, and she was crying harder now.

"—and who one day will be my wife," he said. "God willing."

And then he kissed her again and broke away, saying that he was leaving first thing in the morning. "I'll be back for you after the war," he promised. "I'll sort everything out with Helena after all this business is over."

It would be a brief war, he said; the Brits and French would blow Hitler's army to smithereens, and then he would dissolve his marriage to Helena for real and be with Maude forever. He would think of her constantly during the war, he said; it would help him get through it.

"But after the war, how will you know where I am?" she wanted to know. "How will you find me?"

"Wherever you are, don't worry, I'll find you," he assured her, and then there were voices in the distance, people coming through the courtyard. "Oh, I almost forgot, this is for you," Stephen said, thrusting the brown paper package at her. And then without another word Stephen slipped away into the night, leaving Maude to stand among the silent, expressionless statuary for a few more minutes.

A little while later, once again sitting on her bed in her room, Maude snipped the rough twine of the package with a pair of nail scissors and tore open the brown paper, and there before her was Stephen's gift: to her astonishment it was his beloved, well-worn copy of the poems of A. L. Slayton. A red silk bookmark was slipped inside, marking the page that held *their* poem, "The Rose and the Stag." And on the flyleaf, he had written the following:

To my dear Maude,
Because I won't be needing this for a while. Read these poems while I'm gone, and one day we shall read them again together.

　　　　　　With all my heart,
　　　　　　Stephen

Maude cried herself to sleep that night, the old, worn book pressed against her like a lover.

Though Oxford, like all cities in England, was very vulnerable during the war, Hitler never did drop his bombs here; word had it that he coveted the university too much for that, imagining that one day all of this grandeur would be his. As the capital city, London, of course, was most at risk, but Maude quickly talked Edith into volunteering for the war effort with her at a hospital outside London. Through a friend of Edith's father, who had a very successful surgery on Harley Street, both girls were immediately admitted into the rigorous nurses' training program at the Brackett-on-Heath Hospital.

What a different universe this was from the gentility and ancient traditions of Oxford. Inside the hospital, you could never tell whether it was night or day; the lighting was always the same, a grim yellowish white, a color that reminded Maude of old bones. The head teaching nurse, Miss Patterson, demonstrated no affection for her students and never praised, only criticized. It was grueling labor, practiced on real live patients, children who had been brought in with stomachaches that turned out to be burst appendixes needing extraction, or old men who had been struck by streetcars. These poor people, Maude thought as she created a sterile field for surgery, they had no idea that they were putting themselves in the hands of someone who knew so little.

But as time passed, Maude found she began to know more and more and to become confident assisting at procedures. Studying at night with Edith in their tiny nursing students' quarters in a quiet wing of the hospital—so different from their beautiful rooms at Oxford—she and Edith quizzed each other on neuroanatomy, on the musculoskeletal system, on profuse bleeding and its treatment. There was an overwhelming amount of information to absorb, and Maude knew that if she made one mistake, she might cost someone his life. She longed for the cadences of "The Rose and the Stag" and wished more than anything that she was back in Stephen's study on a peaceful afternoon, lying in his arms again.

Edith, of course, knew all about Stephen now; she'd known since the beginning of the war, because it had been impossible for Maude to hide the truth any longer.

"Do you think I'm immoral?" she asked Edith one night.

Edith didn't answer right away, and then finally she said, "I guess every individual has a different perception of morality. Like the Germans, I suppose. A young German soldier figures that he's doing the honorable thing, doesn't he? Fighting for his country. Obeying his government. Is that immoral?"

"I don't honestly know," said Maude.

"Falling in love with a man who loves you—a man whose own wife makes him miserable," said Edith. "Well, I guess you could say it's immoral. But you could also say it was very kind. It depends on your perspective."

"If someone told me the story of me and Stephen," said Maude, "I'd probably tend to take the immorality view. I mean, I feel guilty about the situation, but there's something larger at work too. Something that makes me feel I have a *right* to be with him. That it was meant to be."

It was a relief to be able to discuss Stephen with her roommate as they lay on their narrow cots in nurses' quarters. Edith had quickly married her boyfriend Ned Waterstone two days before he'd gone off to join the RAF, and the thought of one man somewhere at sea and the other in the air made both Maude and Edith feel how precarious all of life was and how the most they had at any given point was the ability to wish, or pray, that everything would turn out all right in the end.

And when *would* the end come? No one knew how long the war would last, or how severe it would be. But fairly soon the doors of Brackett-on-Heath opened to let in soldiers who'd been injured in battle and been flown home for treatment, or else to die.

None of Nurse Patterson's lectures about wartime injury could possibly have prepared Maude for what she was about to witness. Young men, handsome, faces twisted up in agony, hanging on to life, bloody, blind, hallucinating, all of this was spread before her like some terrible dream that you cannot wake up from, and which instead you keep sinking deeper and deeper into. And in each soldier's face she saw Stephen. She imagined him lying on a stretcher. She saw herself cleansing his wounds, cradling his head in her lap, and whenever she entertained these fantasies it was hard to go on, then harder not to.

For these men *needed* girls like Maude and Edith, untrained though they were. No, they really weren't girls anymore, she realized, they were women now. Women who were tired and overworked, and yet who kept working hour after hour, swiftly striding down the yellow hospital hallway and into the operating theater, scrubbing up and doing whatever needed to be done.

One of the doctors, a surgeon named Allen Drake, was particularly kind to Maude, stopping her from time to time in the staff lunchroom to ask how she was getting along. "Have you settled in well enough?" he asked.

He was a very tall man of thirty, thin, with black hair slicked back off his forehead and striking features, a former cricket champion at Cambridge, she'd heard. Though he was usually thought of as quiet and reserved, he was open and welcoming around Maude. "I've settled in fine, thank you," she said, "but do you mind if I ask you something?"

"Not at all," said Allen Drake.

"How do you . . . do it?" Maude wanted to know.

"Do what?"

"How do you see such terrible things day after day," she asked, "and just proceed as if everything were normal. These soldiers. How do you cope?"

Allen thought about this for a moment. "It's strange, isn't it," he said. "My father was a surgeon in the Great War, and he saw more atrocities than you or I could even imagine. The men who have come through Brackett-on-Heath so far—well, this is just a taste. This is *nothing.* I used to ask Father how he managed, and he shrugged and told me that the more terrible the things he witnessed, the more that life itself became dearer to him, more extraordinary." Allen Drake smiled and shrugged. "I imagine," he said, "that you and I are going to have very extraordinary lives."

Maude really liked Allen and was comforted by their conversations, but a few days later when he asked her if she'd like to go out to dinner that night after he was off duty, she became flustered. It was clear to her that he was interested in her, and that their dinner would constitute a date.

"I'm sorry," Maude said, "but I'm really not free."

"Ah, I see," said Allen. "Bad luck for me, eh?"

Maude smiled kindly at him. Allen appeared dejected, and he fiddled for a moment with the bell of his stethoscope. "Tell me, is it . . . someone in the service?" he wanted to know.

"Yes," Maude admitted. "He's in the Royal Navy." She got a small thrill saying those words, for they sounded so crisply important, so heroic. She thought of Stephen in uniform, standing at the rail on some battleship, though of course she had no idea where he really was.

"I understand," Allen said. "Oh, well." He paused a moment. "But look here, Maude," he said. "If things ever change, well, you know I'm here, all right?"

"They won't change," she said quietly.

"You love this fellow," the doctor said somberly, and Maude nodded.

"Well, then, good luck to both of you," Allen mumbled, and then he quickly retreated into doctors' quarters, and after that day their relationship became notably cooler. He nodded to her from time to time and spoke to her briefly, but he was never as welcoming anymore; she didn't blame him.

Maude saw him chatting up one of the other nurses, a small, outgoing woman from Kentish Town named Valerie, and the following evening she watched them leave the hospital together, heading out into the night and laughing.

Laughter was so rare these days. The wards mostly contained sounds of pain and unhappiness, broken up now and again by scratchy voices on the radio, speaking with urgency about the British army, and the German army, and dire predictions for the future.

In February came the first blackout, with every single light in and around London ordered to be extinguished at night. The entire hospital remained in the dark after sunset, and Maude patrolled the wards in the darkness, making her way from bed to bed, quietly asking "Mr. . . . Wainthrop, is that you?" And then waiting for a reply, and moving on to the next bed, grasping a hand to give comfort to the next man lying there.

The metal-railed beds kept filling; the war, which had taken shape so slowly and

8

amorphously all around Britain, was now
as real as the fragile, broken men who kept
arriving by ambulance each day. Still, none
of them was Stephen, thank God. Stephen
stayed vivid in Maude's mind; he never
faded, though she had no photographs of
him and no letters. He never became a
shadowy figure, a half-person, but remained extremely real to her, and when
she needed a sudden dose of him, she
would steal away to her tiny room and pull
out Stephen's copy of A. L. Slayton's poetry, reading "The Rose and the Stag" out
loud until she felt him there beside her,
reading the poem too.

One afternoon, Maude had a break, and
she took a bus into London to buy a coat,
which she needed badly. Edith was working today and couldn't switch shifts with
another nurse, so Maude went alone. It
was a frozen day, with an icy rain falling
and a sea of black umbrellas raised against
the downpour, and as the bus pulled into
the city, Maude was sorry she'd come.
London was so grim, with newspaper
headlines in boldface and people scam-
pering past on errands that appeared joyless. It was possible to imagine London

being bombed, Maude realized with un-
easiness. All these old buildings, the
palaces and the towers, and Big Ben letting the city know whatever fateful hour
was arriving—she could see them all being
struck, the ceilings collapsing, the black
smoke billowing, the screams coming from
all around.

Tears filled Maude's eyes, as though
London had been bombed already, as
though she was witnessing actual destruction instead of a very vivid fantasy. She
was hungry, she realized. Food was being
rationed now, and Maude had made sure
that she had her coupons with her when
she left the hospital so she could buy a
spot of tea and some cake in a little shop
somewhere after she was done shopping.
But as she walked through the streets, so
many shops were closed, or empty, and a
feeling of foreboding swept across her,
sending Maude suddenly into the far
brighter, more cheerful interior of Harrods.
But the department store was far emptier
than usual too, and none of the shoppers
had a leisurely quality to them; everyone
was in and out, hurrying back to their

homes, worrying, planning, preparing for uncertainty.

Stephen had been correct that Maude's brown cloth coat was ridiculous, but now it was the coldest winter in half a century, and she had to have something truly warm, something unflatteringly thick that would protect her against the wind. Maude was standing in the deserted Women's Overcoats department, quickly riffling through the rack for whatever coats in her size remained, when she saw a familiar face across the way.

Immediately she knew that it was Stephen's wife, Helena.

Maude felt sick and guilty and frightened all at once. The two women had been standing across from each other, pushing coats on hangers along a squeaky rack in order to find something suitable, and now they had lifted their heads and were looking into each other's eyes at the same moment. It was startling, disturbing, but there was no way around it.

"Hello," Maude said.

"Hello," said Helena Kendall slowly. "Do we know each other?"

"You may not remember me," Maude

said. "I'm Maude Latham. We met in Oxford, Mrs. Kendall. Your husband was my tutor."

Helena paused, then nodded. "Yes, of course," she said. "Now I remember."

She looked extremely wan, Maude noticed, her face free of makeup, the lips pale, the eyes as heavy-lidded as they'd been last time. Instead of a fancy hat with a feather stuck into it, though, she wore a simple cashmere hood that contributed to her haunted, frail appearance.

"I'm looking for a coat," Maude said lamely, when all she desperately wanted to say was: *Even though I have no right to know this, please tell me everything you know about Stephen—where he is, how he is, whether he's safe, when I can see him again.*

"I am too," said Stephen's wife. "Though the selection is pathetic, damn war."

"Aren't you supposed to be evacuated?" Maude asked.

Helena shrugged. "Technically, I am," she said. "I left Oxford when the war started and went to Gloryhead, my family's estate in Devon. But I've been restless in the country, and every now and then I

sneak into London to cheer myself up."
She paused a moment. "Look, would you
like to get a cup of tea?" she asked.

Maude was startled; how strange to be
sharing a casual and friendly cup of tea
with her lover's wife. In retrospect, she
supposed that she ought to have said no,
ought to have made some excuse and not
behaved so hypocritically, yet just the idea
of finding one thing out about Stephen was
enough to land her in the tearoom of Harrods across a table from Mrs. Stephen
Kendall.

They sat by the window, though they
could have had their choice of tables; the
place was empty but for one lone, sad-
looking man nursing a glass of lemon
squash. When the waiter came over, Helena gave their order without first consult-
ing Maude: two cress sandwiches; two
plates of rocket with salad cream; two iced
cakes; and two cups of tea with milk and
sugar.

The waiter blinked nervously. "Sorry,
love," he said apologetically, "I'll need to
see your coupons."

Helena sighed and reached into her
purse, pulling out a ration book and tearing

off the remaining two coupons. "There," she said, "it's all I've got with me." Maude quickly followed suit, turning over her own coupons.

"I'm sorry, ladies," the waiter repeated, "I can't give you all those items you asked for. The sandwiches, perhaps, and some tea, but no salad and no cakes."

"Oh, for God's sake," said Helena angrily, "I'm a very wealthy woman. This rationing business is nonsense. Please bring me what I ordered."

The waiter, embarrassed, held firm, and finally Maude softly said, "It's all right, Helena, I'm not very hungry anyway." Which wasn't true, really, but she was embarrassed too by Helena's imperious behavior, and frankly she didn't care what they ate. She just wanted to hear about Stephen.

Helena sighed and waved the waiter away. "Very well," she said. "Go along then."

When the sandwiches and tea arrived, the two women sat awkwardly and ate. Maude told her about working in Brackett-on-Heath, and Helena spoke vaguely about wishing that she herself could help

the war effort, but that her "nerves" prevented her from being very useful.

"I've always been a victim of my nerves,"
she said. "Ever since I was a child. When I
met Stephen, the first thing I noticed about
him was how tender and caring he was. He
actually seemed to take pleasure from seeing that I was all right, from helping me
when I had an attack of nerves. It was a
great comfort, you have no idea."

Oh, yes, I do, thought Maude. But what
she said was, "Have you . . . heard from
him?" She tried to make her voice sound
casual and careless.

"Well, not directly, but I've been informed of his whereabouts," said Helena.
"He's in Intelligence, you see. And those
fellows, from what I gather, have the great-
est security restrictions placed on them; no
one can know where they are or what
they're doing. I've been informed that he's
safe for now, but that's all I know."

"I see," said Maude. *Intelligence.* It was
a perfect word to apply to Stephen Kendall. He was, above all else, *intelligent,* and
Maude imagined him off somewhere sending coded messages, or deciphering messages intercepted from the SS. She saw

him on a ship, sitting at one of those radio sets, headphones in his ears, listening, tapping out something with his fingers. She was so happy to have received this information from Helena; it made her whole day, it lit up London for her, brought it out of its gloom and fear and vulnerability.

"So, Maude, tell me," said Helena suddenly, "did I give you what you wanted to know?"

Maude stared at her, trying to read Stephen's wife's face. "Yes, yes, you did," she finally said.

"Good," said Helena Kendall. And then Helena smiled. It was a peculiar smile, thin and unfriendly, and now Maude was certain that Helena *knew,* and that Helena wanted her to know she knew. It was a moment of understanding between the two women. They weren't friends, and never would be.

Maude had never had a rival before. She didn't really know how she was supposed to behave around her rival, but her instinct, oddly, was to be kind. For she knew that, even though Helena Kendall was still married to Stephen, and Helena, not she, was the one who was entitled to receive infor-

mation about his whereabouts and his situation, Maude was the one who could
honestly lay claim to Stephen's heart. It
had been a long time since Helena had
loved Stephen, and a long time since they
had made love. All that existed between
the husband and wife was a deep, mutual
chill.

He needs so much more than that,
Maude would have liked to say to
Stephen's wife. *He needs someone to love
him, and I can do that, even if you can't.
You had your chance, and you didn't take
it. Please don't hate me.*

But of course Helena Kendall hated her;
she had every right to, and Maude knew
that. She couldn't justify her relationship
with Stephen, a married man, and she
knew that her own parents would have
been ashamed of her if they'd found out
about it. But it had happened, and it was a
reality, and it wasn't going to go away.
Even Helena Kendall seemed to know that.

"Well," Stephen's wife was saying, "I
should be getting back to Gloryhead. And I
guess you'll want to go back to Women's
Overcoats now."

"Yes, I do need a coat," Maude murmured faintly.

They stood together and left the tearoom. It was only when they'd walked back out into the main part of the store, with its gleaming floors and distantly ringing chimes calling some employee to another department, that Helena casually inquired, "Oh, one more thing. Perhaps you'll still need a scarf. Unless, of course, you finally bought one for yourself?"

A scarf. So Helena remembered that Maude had been wearing Stephen's scarf that day almost a year ago. She'd filed it away, knowing at the time that it was significant, and now she was bringing it up to make absolutely certain that Maude understood she was no fool.

"No," said Maude. "I never did buy one."

The two women regarded each other for a last moment in the light of Harrods, standing together by the glass counter that sold sewing scissors and pincushions and notions. It seemed like hours that they stood there, Helena Kendall in all her cool, brittle beauty, and Maude just looking at her, flustered, working to keep her composure, telling herself that at this moment she herself was the one with the "attack of nerves" but that it would pass soon enough.

And then it was Helena who finally said, "Well, good-bye then."

"Good-bye," said Maude.

The two women shook hands, and though Mrs. Stephen Kendall's hand was bare and ungloved, it was anything but warm.

CHAPTER FIVE

She couldn't pretend that the encounter with Stephen's wife wasn't extremely disturbing. Whenever Maude pictured Helena Kendall's face now she felt both chilled and guilty, so she quickly replaced the image with one of Stephen, and then everything seemed all right for a while. Though he wasn't her husband—though he was someone else's husband still—she knew he would someday be hers, and that if God forbid he were to die, she would be as devastated as any authentic widow.

But he wouldn't die, because she wouldn't let him.

It was this willed sensation of omnipotence that allowed Maude Latham to get through that first long, frozen winter, and then the joyless spring that followed. This season, the thawing of the snow and ice on the roads didn't contain within it a hopefulness. Why were the birds singing in the linden and poplar trees that lined the front walkway to the hospital? They had no reason to sing, no right. No one else was singing; no one else had moments of careless release.

When the war had started in September, the prime minister, Neville Chamberlain, had told the British people, "It is evil things that we shall be fighting against—brute force, bad faith, injustice, oppression, and persecution." Maude knew that all of this still held true, but it didn't make it any easier when the person you loved most in the world was among those doing the fighting against brute force, injustice, and the like. This was a selfish and self-absorbed thought at a time when everyone in the entire country needed to be thinking not of themselves, but of their country, and what they could contribute.

Still, she was doing what she could for England; her contribution wasn't really at issue. Though it had been her feelings for Stephen that had kept her from fleeing for America when Britain entered the war, her initial motivation was now irrelevant. She'd become a good nurse, a competent and intuitive one if not exactly stellar, and her presence at Brackett-on-Heath was urgently needed. Maude spent all her days and nights on the third-floor trauma ward, taking care of injured soldiers who were brought in, it seemed, in bulk, backed up into the hospital driveway and carried out like truckloads of linens. It was an enormous task, impossible for the relatively small staff to manage. There weren't enough doctors and nurses to attend to all the men who had been transported home by train and truck from battle, especially after May ended and the beaten British army returned from Dunkirk, picked up on French beaches and ferried home by English boats. Many of the injured were brought directly to Brackett-on-Heath and other hospitals.

Churchill, the new prime minister, spoke sternly and stirringly, warning the British that the Battle of France was lost, and that the Battle of Britain was about to begin. Everyone tried to steel themselves for what was coming, but Maude didn't even know what that really meant. How did you prepare for something so terrible? No one had been able to stop what was happening on the Continent; how could the British defend themselves from Hitler if no one else could? Surely giving up their aluminum pots and pans to make aeroplane parts, as housewives throughout the country were urged to do, wasn't going to save the day.

The months slowly ticked by, and though England was cowering in wait, Maude was far too busy to be truly frightened. Whenever she had a quiet moment she thought of Stephen. And then in September came the blitz, the nightly attacks on London that sent the entire population of the city—or whoever was left and wasn't off fighting, or lying dead in a battlefield, or evacuated to the countryside to hide trembling beneath a haystack—into air-raid shelters or into the Underground, despite the government insistences that they shouldn't go there.

The sirens roared, and everyone scrambled for cover again and again. The bombs fell, a hailstorm of the ordinary explosive kind, as well as those incendiary bombs that simply set on fire whatever they touched. Ceilings caved in, people were

crushed and families destroyed, and hundreds upon hundreds of ordinary civilians—
housewives, milkmen, clerks—wound up in
Brackett-on-Heath. London at night, that
city in the near distance which, during the
day, Maude could see the tips of from the
roof of the hospital, became a terrified
place of darkness, with all traffic lights
masked to show only small crosses of
color, and all car headlights masked to reveal slits of light. Churchill ought to order all
the citizens to be masked too, Maude
thought, so no one would have to witness
this terrible and endless destruction. Even
smoking was banned on the streets for a
while, but still London gave off a distinctive
glow of light at night that couldn't be
missed, and still the bombs kept falling and
the injured kept filling the wards, keeping
the nurses and doctors sleepless.

Once Maude found herself drifting off in
the middle of sewing up a man's leg, and
Nurse Patterson had to call her name
harshly. After that experience Maude
forced herself awake, pouring so much
coffee down her throat that she felt jittery
and strange. But life, now, was jittery and
strange; becoming overcaffeinated would

only put her in harmony with the world she inhabited.

Then one night in spring, at 4 A.M., an uncharacteristically quiet night, Maude and Edith were both asleep in their cots, which was also uncharacteristic, when there was a rapid knock on their door.

"Come in," Maude called automatically, rising from the cot.

There at the door stood two men in uniform. They were at attention, heads tipped slightly up, clearly here on official business. She was half-awake, but still she almost fainted looking at them, for two men in uniform in the middle of the night was never a good sign. *Stephen,* she thought, *oh God, not this.*

"Nurse Edith Waterstone?" one of the men asked, and his voice was surprisingly gentle.

"No," said Maude. "She's inside. May I ask what this is about?"

"We'd like to talk to her, if we may," said the other man, his voice also kind.

And then Maude realized through her disoriented haze that the uniforms were RAF, and of course Edith's husband, Ned, was a pilot now, flying bombing missions over German skies.

"What's going on, Maude?" Edith asked, coming to the door with her pale pink robe pulled around her. She saw the RAF men standing there looking at her, and she registered the compassion in their eyes, and then she looked back and forth between them and quietly, hoarsely, said, "Is it Ned?"

"May we come inside?" the first man asked, and Edith started to sink down to the floor and Maude caught her, held her, gathered her friend against her while the two men made motions to help, but all of it was useless.

There was nothing to do for Edith, no way to help her. Ned Waterstone, a biology student at Oxford, a friendly, athletic, uncomplicated man whom Edith had passionately loved, had been shot down on a mission over Frankfurt. He was twenty years old.

Throughout the rest of the night, Maude stayed up with Edith and held her friend while she wept and talked about Ned, their plans, the kind of person he was, the way her entire life had suddenly changed shape before her.

"You think it can't happen to you," said Edith during a brief break in the tears, "and then it does. You think, somehow, that the man you love has some magic protection around him. As though your love will keep him safe, like some kind of talisman. You can't really believe that anyone so good could be taken. If Hitler knew, if he just knew what kind of a man Ned was, a man who loved people, and wanted to be a scientist, and who was good to his mother—" She stopped and sighed. "Well, it wouldn't have made a difference, I know," she said. "Hitler couldn't care less. Winning is everything, right? Forget about the human faces wearing those uniforms. Forget about the people who loved those soldiers, and who will never get over their deaths, ever."

At Maude's urging, Edith managed to get a few days off from her job at the hospital, in order to go home to the countryside and be with her family. Maude even wondered if Edith would resign; how could she work with such a heavy heart? How could she possibly think of anything but poor, lost Ned? Yet after three days with her family, three days of sitting on the window seat and looking out over the fields and letting her solicitous mother cook stews and puddings for her, she had had enough. Edith reappeared at the hospital, changed out of her street clothes and into uniform, and announced that she was ready to work again.

"I have to go on," she said. "There's really nothing else to do, is there?"

That was what it was like, this war; terrible things happened and then you just went on. There was nothing else to do but become completely absorbed in the events of the day, for they were real, they existed, and they couldn't be ignored, even if you were suffused with grief. Everyone, it seemed, had lost someone; everyone suffered, and then somehow they woke up the next morning and climbed out of bed.

When Edith returned she was a little thinner, her skin slightly ashen, but she insisted she was perfectly capable of doing her work, and in fact she threw herself into the job with a new energy and diligence that Maude hadn't seen before. Maude took it upon herself to look after Edith, to make sure that whenever Edith felt an unbearable curtain of melancholy coming over her, Maude was there to comfort her, and distract her if necessary with endless games of snap and Cluedo. And then, eventually, with the crossword puzzle from the Sunday *Times,* which Maude had grown quite good at.

One of the doctors at the hospital, the elderly Dr. Manning, had taught Maude to solve the puzzles. At first she'd been completely mystified by the clues, which bore no resemblance to the clues in American crossword puzzles. British clues contained puns and anagrams and were extremely tricky and deliberately maddening to someone who grew up with simpler American puzzles.

One of the clues that Dr. Manning showed her read "A hot, frilled figure of furor, we hear?" And the answer, he told her, was "Adolf Hitler."

"But why?" Maude asked. "You'll think I'm extremely thick, but I have no idea of how you arrived at that answer."

And then Dr. Manning explained that if you made an anagram out of the letters in "a hot, frilled," you would get "Adolf Hitler."

"But what about the rest of the clue?"

asked Maude. "It doesn't make any sense to me. 'Figure of furor, we hear?' "

Dr. Manning smiled, clearly enjoying explaining how these puzzles worked; in England, it seemed, everybody and their six-year-old niece knew how to solve a cryptic puzzle. But Americans were in the dark. "You see," he said, "whenever the clue includes the words 'we hear,' that means it's going to have a word in it that sounds like another word. In this case, that word is *furor.*"

Maude thought about it for a moment. "I see," she said. "The 'figure of furor' is the same as the figure of 'führer'! Adolf Hitler!"

"Exactly," said Dr. Manning. "Fairly soon you'll be entering the London *Times*'s contest and winning a few pounds."

Now, Maude and Edith sat in the lounge whenever they had a few moments to themselves and worked on the crossword puzzle. Maude had gotten to the point where she could solve many of the clues fairly rapidly, although sometimes the very British quality to these puzzles—their reliance on the solver's knowledge of members of parliament thirty years earlier, or obscure rivers in the far reaches of the

etimes they were from her parents,
lly her father.

dear girl,
u are now embarked on a mission
t your mother and I can only gape
from afar, quite literally. While it's
ious you're behaving in a very un-
e manner, it's also obvious that you
brave. And that is something that
never had the opportunity to be,
gh I wish I had. I'd also like to say
that it's occurred to me that you
t have some other reasons for
ng on in Britain now. And if that's
you don't need to tell me what
are. But just know that I've come
spect your choices, though they
eep your mother and me wide
e at night.

Much love,
Father

ch Maude quickly replied,

ather,
u are right, there is another rea-
still here. (And even if there

country (whose names woul
be unscrambled and dec
completely . . . "clueless," a

But the puzzles were
pleasant wordplay; they he
of something other than I
Edith sat side by side on
or on the old, cracked ma
enport in the lounge, and
clue after clue until they f
heads would break. Ec
with words, and none o
a little while, was "Ned
was grateful. Distrac
Maude get through tha
death of Ned, she real
stakes, had been a st
Stephen was up ag
wouldn't protect him
that he loved poetr
Maude.

Whenever the pos
that there was a le
mailbox, Maude fel
citement that some
Stephen, even thou
he would never be
letters never were

Som
usua

My
Yo
tha
at
obv
wis
are
I've
thou
here
migl
stayi
true,
they
to re
still k
awak

To whi

Dear F
Yes, yo
son I'r

weren't another reason, I would still stay on, for I am needed more desperately than I think you can imagine.) I don't want to say too much at this point, but I will tell you that my life has grown complicated over the last two years, though in wonderful ways. And I hope to be able to tell you and Mother all about it (and about him) one of these days.

Much love from
Maude, "British Trauma Nurse"
(can you believe it?)

She hadn't seen or spoken to Stephen for over one year, and yet time seemed distorted to her; it might have been one month, or ten years. Everything had the strange unreality and grotesque waviness of a life lived inside a fun house mirror. The war only deepened, and that meant that Stephen was no closer to coming home, no closer to leaving his wife and being with her.

But then one day, with no warning, she heard from him. He did not come in person or send a letter; instead, he sent another member of the Royal Navy to pay Maude a

visit. It was late October the day that Lieutenant Jared Thomson came to Brackett-
on-Heath. Another winter was brewing in
England; another terrible winter they would
all have to get through. Nobody paid any
attention to the lieutenant when he strode
through the hospital halls; this place was
crawling with servicemen.

"Hello," said the man to the student
nurse at the desk. "I'm looking for Nurse
Maude Latham. I was told at the front desk
that she'd be here. Is she?"

"Oh, sure, she's around here somewhere." The student nurse looked up and
called out, "Maude, you have a visitor,"
and in a moment Maude stood up from a
chair on the far side of the hallway, where
she'd been taking a brief break from her
shift, sipping tea and filling in today's
crossword puzzle from the newspaper.

A visitor. This was the first time she'd
ever had one since she'd come to the hospital, and when Maude peered down the
corridor and saw a man in a naval uniform
leaning against the nurses' station, she
was seized by a terrible fear, remembering
the late-night knock on the door from the
RAF. Clutching her newspaper tightly, her

steps quickened, her rubber nurse's heels squeaking on the shiny dark lino, and her heart thudding dully inside her until finally she found herself running toward him, running the way the trauma team ran when there was an urgent call to the operating theater. But then the man looked at her, saw that she was running toward him, and he did the strangest thing: he smiled.

"Nurse Latham?" he asked, and his voice was warm and welcoming. Surely he couldn't be about to inform her that Stephen had been killed; her heart slowed slightly, and she was able to calm herself down a little. "My name is Lieutenant Jared Thomson," he said. "I'm sure you're wondering why I've come."

"Well, yes," said Maude. "I was, actually."

"I've been asked to bring you a letter from a friend."

"Do you mean Stephen Kendall?" Maude asked quietly.

Lieutenant Thomson nodded. "Commander Kendall asked me to deliver the letter to you personally."

Commander Kendall; how strange that sounded, how important and official. She wondered for a moment how Stephen had found out what hospital she was working in, but then she remembered her awkward meeting with Helena Kendall at Harrods. Helena must have mentioned it to Stephen.

"Is he all right?" Maude asked carefully.

"Well, actually, I'm afraid he's been injured," the lieutenant replied.

"What sort of injury?" asked Maude, frightened.

"It's his lower leg. Shrapnel had to be removed by the medics, and there was some nerve damage."

"Oh no. But he's . . . all right?" Maude asked.

"You mean will he live?" asked Lieutenant Thomson. "Oh yes, he'll live. I was told he's expected to make a full recovery, but that it may take some time."

"I'm so relieved," said Maude, momentarily forgetting that she ought to appear composed and casual right now. Stephen, after all, was just "a friend." That was what he had told Jared Thomson, and Maude understood that it was imperative not to reveal the truth. The Royal Navy wouldn't look kindly on adulterous behavior by one of its commanders.

"I was assigned to accompany Commander Kendall back home to meet his wife in Oxford," Lieutenant Thomson went on.

"From where?" Maude asked.

He shook his head. "Sorry. I'm not at liberty to say."

"That's all right. I'll take what I can get. You see, he and I are good friends, and I haven't heard one word about his whereabouts or his situation. This is the first news I've gotten since he went away."

"I know," said Jared Thomson softly, and just as Maude had understood from Helena Kendall's coldness that Helena knew Maude was in love with Stephen, so did Maude understand from Lieutenant Thomson's warmth that *he* knew about the situation too.

He looked evenly at Maude as he spoke, and then he nodded once, reassuringly. "Commander Kendall asked if I would mind staying on in Oxford for a few days. He told me it would be very useful to him, since he'd need lots of assistance getting up and down the stairs, and his wife isn't strong enough to help him."

"So you're staying there?" Maude said

with forced nonchalance. "At Stephen's house?"

"Yes. He'll be there for a few weeks, perhaps a month, and then after he's recovered he'll go back to his post in the navy." He paused, then added, "Oxford is such a beautiful place, though of course it's a bit of a ghost town now. But before the war it must have been wonderful."

"Oh yes," said Maude. "Completely wonderful."

"I can't even imagine what it would have been like to have studied at the university," said Thomson. "I hear they're always putting on terrific productions of plays there."

"Oh yes," said Maude. "Last year they did a wonderful *Volpone,* and of course there's plenty of Shakespeare."

"That sounds wonderful," said Thomson. "I'd give anything to go to Oxford and be in plays there. Me, I went right from Gordonstoun into the Royal Navy. The sea has been my education."

"Well, that's quite an education," said Maude politely, though she was becoming increasingly anxious to see the letter from Stephen. But she couldn't very well say, "Look, hand it over already, will you?"

But then he did. He reached into an inside pocket of his uniform and pulled out a long white envelope. On it, in a slightly shaky version of Stephen's handwriting, was Maude's name. Simply seeing his handwriting gave her a shiver, sent a powerful memory through her: Stephen's writing, Stephen's hand holding a pen, Stephen's arm, his shoulder, his face.

Maude took the envelope and held it. "Thank you," she said. "Now I'm awfully sorry, Lieutenant Thomson, but I have to get back to my patients. If you'd like some hot tea, there's some in the staff lounge. Please do have some. You've come all this way, and I'm very grateful."

"Thank you, I will," he said.

"Are you going back?" she asked. "Back to wherever you've been stationed?" What she really meant was, of course, *wherever you and Stephen have been stationed.*

"Yes," he said. "In a few days."

"Well, good luck to you then," she said softly. "And maybe when this whole thing is over, you can be a student at Oxford after all."

"Maybe," Jared Thomson said, "though

at this rate I'll be one of the oldest under-
graduates ever."

"I'm sure you'll have plenty of company,"
said Maude.

They smiled warmly at each other and
shook hands again. Then Lieutenant
Thomson glanced down briefly at the
newspaper in Maude's hand that was
folded back to the crossword. He saw that
the grid was mostly filled in already.

"That's impressive," he said.

"Oh, yes, I'm really demonstrating my
Oxford education, aren't I?" Maude said,
and then they both laughed. Then Maude
hurried to her quarters, sat down on her
tightly made cot, and looked down at
Stephen's letter. She savored it for a moment, imagined its contents, its carefully
written, beautiful words that she'd been
waiting for all year. Of course, the war
wasn't over yet, not even close, but
Stephen was injured and home and was
therefore allowed to send her a note, since
he wasn't in a classified location from
where his letter could be traced. She sat
and held his letter, feeling the cool paper of
the envelope in her hands, the envelope

that Stephen had held. Then she took a breath and opened it.

"Maude," it began.

"I've only a moment to write. Helena is quite nearby, and I must attend to her. As you will have heard by now from Lt. Thomson, I've been hurt, and the pain is severe at times, and the pills I've been given by the medics affect my powers of concentration. This letter will be rather artless, but I hope to make a point. Perhaps I shall just leave it to A. L. Slayton." And then on the next page, he had written out "The Rose and the Stag." Except, she noticed with surprise, it wasn't the whole poem, with its satisfying union of the lovers, but just the final stanza, in which the rose has her terrible dream:

> Her lamp was still lit but he no longer
>   saw,
> For he had chang'd o'er winter, the
>   way all stags do,
> hardening in the wild.
> And she was flower to him no more,
> but mere woman, imperfect.
> She could not believe he could be so
>   cruel

Yet he left her there, a rose for all
    eternity,
then turn'd and leapt away.

And then below it, Stephen simply
signed his name.

At first she didn't understand. And then
she did.

He had left her. It was over.

She had no idea why—just the way, in
the rose's dream, she can't quite believe
the stag has left her. Of course, in the full
version of the poem, the stag doesn't *really*
leave the rose at all; she has just dreamt he
does. But to include only this section, "to
make a point," as Stephen had written,
could only be interpreted one way. What
had she done? Nothing, nothing, of
course, how could she have done anything? He hadn't seen her for over a year,
yet in that time, like the stag in the dream,
he had apparently changed, hardened. The
war had done that to him. He was hardened and had somehow fallen out of love
with her. Coming home wounded and seeing his fragile wife again had probably reminded him of his obligations to Helena,
which mixed with his own cooled feelings.

Whatever the reason, he was no longer hers. Theirs had been an Oxford romance, like many before it, thriving in the beauty and tranquility of the university, the long afternoons, lingering over books, a drink together, a walk along the Thames, a brief trip to London—pre-blitz London, with its buildings that hadn't been bombed yet—to stay at the Rose and Stag, a place Maude hadn't even been able to bring herself to look at since Stephen left.

She bunched the letter up into a ball, crushed it inside her fist, and allowed herself to cry. It was strange; she'd gotten so proficient at *not crying* since she'd been at Brackett-on-Heath. She simply couldn't cry in front of her patients, for then they too would feel worse about their situation, and would become convinced it was hopeless. She always had to be positive, upbeat, swift and professional and reassuring. "Let's have a look at that now," she'd say to a soldier who lay bleeding; even though, of course, she didn't really have to take a close look to know what she would find.

Patients had died, and she hadn't cried. Just a month earlier there had been a fifteen-year-old boy who had arrived with a head injury after his house was bombed. His name was Nigel Pierce, and despite the pain he was in, he was funny and wry, reminding Maude of her younger brother, James, whom she hadn't seen since she sailed over on the *Queen Mary.* Whenever Maude walked past Nigel's room, he knew it was she by the particular squeak of her shoes.

"Your shoes go squeak-*squeeeeak*-squeak," he explained. "Nurse Waterstone's shoes just go squeak-squeak-squeak. And most of the other nurses, I have no idea how their shoes sound because I don't really like them all that well. Nurse Patterson, now her shoes don't squeak at all, do they?"

"I suppose not," Maude admitted. "I've never really thought of it before, but now that I do . . . no, her shoes are completely silent."

"So she can just arrive like a vampire and suck my blood in the middle of the night," said Nigel.

"Oh, do stop," said Maude, laughing. "You'll get me in trouble."

"Sometimes I lie here," Nigel said after a

moment, "and just listen for that extralong squeak that tells me it's going to be you. And whenever it is, I feel very happy. It's the only time, lying here in this miserable place, that I feel that way."

Maude always tried to find an extra moment to spend with Nigel; she brought him newspapers to read and the racing form, and she made sure to give his mother, Mrs. Pierce, a kind, worried woman, daily updates on Nigel's condition. Then one night there was an emergency call summoning several nurses and doctors to Nigel's bed. Without warning, a week after his injury, he'd begun bleeding into his brain. He didn't survive the night.

She wanted to cry; she wanted to scream and pound the walls and tell everyone how unfair and grotesque it was: this lovely boy, who hadn't done anything wrong, who wasn't even old enough to fight in the war, who'd had his whole life ahead of him. But she didn't cry, because when Mrs. Pierce was summoned to the hospital and told about her only son, that lovely boy, she was the one who deserved to cry, and Maude's responsibility was to comfort her. Which she did.

Maude had cried when Ned Waterstone was killed, not because she couldn't help herself but also because she knew that it was all right to cry, it was appropriate. Edith needed her tears as well as her own; Edith needed the solidarity that a crying friend could give. So Maude cried with her a few times, and then she stopped, letting Edith do the rest of the crying, and Maude do the listening.

But now, after the letter from Stephen, there really wasn't a choice about whether or not Maude *ought* to cry. The tears simply came, unbidden. Stephen, the man who had gotten her through this entire year, the man she was patiently waiting for, had dropped her coldly, not even saying he was sorry or trying to explain in depth but simply propping himself up on A. L. Slayton, letting the poet do the explaining. Stephen couldn't be bothered, it seemed.

Goddamn him, and goddamn Maude's innocence for believing that a married man, an officer in the Royal Navy, was still pining away for the young woman he'd slept with back at Oxford, when everything was different. Perhaps he'd slept with other students before; perhaps he was one of those men who did such things. Maude had always known that Stephen's behavior—becoming involved with a student while married—had seemed suspect, if the facts were laid out objectively. But the truth had seemed more complex than that; true, he was married, but his marriage was practically nonexistent. He had a troubled, moody, perhaps mentally ill wife who no longer slept with him or loved him. And he had a young lover, Maude, who was madly in love with him, and who had changed his life, giving actual meaning to the poems he loved.

But Maude had been conned. He had used her, obviously, for his own gratification, and now he was discarding her. Though she should have been angry, the tears came and came, and eventually one of the other nurses sent Edith to the room to find out what was the matter, for Maude's crying jag was audible up and down the corridor.

"It's Stephen," Maude said in explanation when Edith arrived.

"Stephen?" said Edith, and she slowly sat down on the edge of the cot. "What are you saying? Not . . . like Ned?"

"No," said Maude, and wiped her eyes with her handkerchief. "Not at all like Ned. It's just that he doesn't love me anymore. He tells me it's over."

"I can't believe that," said Edith. "He was besotted with you. What about, 'Oh, just wait until the war is over, my love,' et cetera, et cetera. How could he just change his mind like that?"

"How indeed," said Maude. "He quotes the last stanza of 'The Rose and the Stag,' you know, the part with the nightmare, in which he rejects her because he's changed."

"I thought it was a love poem," said Edith, confused.

"It is," said Maude, "if you read the entire thing. But if you just include the last stanza without anything else, then it's a kiss-off letter, don't you see? A 'Dear Jane' letter, as we say in the States. It's Stephen's way of telling me it's over, that he's done with me."

"I just can't believe it," Edith kept saying.

"See for yourself," said Maude, and she handed her the letter.

Edith agreed that the letter seemed unambiguous. "Poor Maude," said Edith.

"You've been so good to me since Ned was killed, and now I can't think of one thing to say to you to make you feel better."

"There's nothing to say," said Maude dully. "This isn't a death. It only feels like one. Nobody has died; I can't expect anyone's condolences. And he wasn't even my husband, Edith, that's the thing. He was nothing to me, just an idea, just a fantasy about what we would have together one day."

"Write to him immediately," said Edith. "Ask him to give you more of an explanation."

But Maude shook her head. "He's made himself clear," she said.

She realized, then, that her tears were gone; she had none left, as though there was only a finite supply of them inside each person, and hers had been used. Maude stood then and pulled open her dresser drawer; inside was Stephen's copy of the poems of A. L. Slayton, the book he had inscribed to her, and which had comforted her throughout the year. She picked it up with two hands and held it against her.

"What are you doing?" asked Edith.

"I'll be right back," Maude said, and then, like someone sleepwalking, she carried the book down the hall to the staff lounge.

There in the corner was the oversize dustbin that the staff tossed all sorts of refuse into throughout the day. And without any hesitation, Maude threw the book into the bin, for she wouldn't need it anymore. There would be no more sitting and mooning over A. L. Slayton's delicate words, no more memories of leaning against Stephen in the light of his study and listening to him read aloud to her. She would never again pick up this book for comfort; the book made her sick now, actually, with all its flowery, suggestive words and their references to love. A. L. Slayton was long dead; he'd lived in another century, another time. His beliefs about love—about two people being right for each other, perfect for each other, and waiting as long as necessary in order to be together—no longer had any relevance. People could wait and wait, Maude knew, and still love passed them by. Some lovers were killed in pointless battle, or else, just as pointlessly, some changed their minds.

It took two willing people to make a couple, not just one. Maude was willing, but Stephen apparently wasn't. She couldn't force him, or beg him; that would be pathetic. There was nothing Maude could do to get Stephen back. He would stay with his fragile wife, and Maude would get on with her life, whatever kind of life it turned out to be. She turned and left the staff lounge, leaving the poems of A. L. Slayton at the bottom of the dustbin, among old newspapers and wrappers from cake cartons and empty tins of beans. She never looked back.

CHAPTER SIX

It was too late. That was the hell of it, as Stephen would have said, but what Stephen would have said no longer mattered. It would have been very tricky getting out of England now, so she was here, and that was that. At the start of the war, Maude had pledged her service to Britain, committing her foreseeable future to the preservation of the empire and the world, as dramatic as that sounded, and for better or worse it was in Britain that she would now remain for the duration.

"For the duration." That was the expression. It was the expression for *everything* these days. It was an awful term, an ugly term, Maude felt. It was a phrase that on the surface simply meant "for as long as this war might last," but it had come to suggest so much more. This war wasn't like other wars; this was an all-or-nothing affair. Even the Great War had ended in a kind of mutual exhaustion, the two sides equally spent, punch-drunk boxers barely standing, holding on to each other for support, each equally unable and unwilling to continue. Not this time. No truce, no treaty, no compromise was going to end this war. Once it had begun in earnest, there was no going back. It wasn't just the Great War all over again, everyone said; it was the Great War *still:* the same two old fighters, off the canvas, out of their corners, shoulders rubbed, smelling salts whiffed, back on the balls of their feet, only this time there was no bell to stop the pounding, the bloodletting, and the flesh-rending. A fight to the finish. Last man standing, and all that. You either won, and your conception of the future of humanity would come to pass, or— well, there was no *or.*

Which made the fight worth fighting. There was no denying that. Never, not once, did Maude doubt that. For that, she was grateful. If you were going to devote your life, possibly sacrifice it, for a greater good, then this was the one to do it for. It wasn't always easy to remember this, when the bombs were dropping and she was sitting in a shelter shoulder to shoulder with Edith, breathing that same gas that always came from where?—the ground? the air? the bombs? who knew where?—and closing her eyes against the same rain of dirt. Even the wounded men in their stretchers and chairs and bandages and pathetic stained pajamas stopped groaning, the better to hear just how close the drumming of the bombs had come. "Pinch me," Edith would whisper, or Maude, and then the other would do so, digging a fingernail into the fleshy thumb pad of her friend's hand, giving her a gift: here is the pain you will think about now, instead.

One Mississippi. Two Mississippi. Three Mississippi.

What did the nurses in a bunker in Berlin count to? Maude wondered. Or, better, here, in London? *One Thames, two Thames*—no, that would never do. It was madness, to count down a war. *This* war, anyway. Which didn't mean you didn't do it. You *did* do it. You did it every day, if need be. You did it, you did it, you did it, you did it, you did it. Because what choice did you have but to do it?

But: What clock were you counting it *against*?

"The duration."

Which was precisely why Maude came to hate that expression so. It took time-lessness, potentially one of the most pleasurable sensations possible—if, say, you were in the arms of a lover—and trans-formed it into a torture.

She should have done it while she could—done everything while she could: get out of England; get out of her affair with Stephen. Sometimes during an air raid, as the first shriek of a siren sounded and she began calmly rounding up the am-bulatory patients in her ward and gently guiding them toward the stairs and down to the shelter, encouraging them to stand, to walk, to wheel or shuffle or hobble or drag, she would think back on the middle of that first night in the Rose and Stag and the ambulance siren that had awakened her, and she would wish that she'd heeded its plea: *get out.*

Stephen had tried to tell her. He'd tried to warn her. She saw that now. They'd sat in the pub that long-ago afternoon, on a weekend when they shouldn't have been thinking about anything but that weekend, and he'd urged her to think about the future. *Be realistic:* that's what he'd said, and Maude, foolishly, had assumed he was talking only about the war.

His voice still echoed, that was true; how could it not? But not his actions, not his essence, not his influence, his insight, his guidance or advice. In the aftermath of the visit from Lieutenant Thomson and the letter he'd delivered, Commander Stephen Kendall of the Royal Navy was worse than dead to Maude. He was *gone.*

Edith, at least, could grieve. She could spend the rest of her life mourning the man who was. She could fall in love again, tell a second husband about the first one, the RAF pilot who would always have a special place in her heart, explain that it was the brief time she'd spent with him that had in fact taught her how to love.

Maude, however, could remember only the man who *wasn't*—wasn't, in the end, what he'd said he was.

Maybe she was being too harsh. Maybe Stephen meant everything he said when he said it, and meant it just the way Maude had thought he'd meant it at the time. *Be realistic:* an honest expression of concern, in anticipation of war, for the safety of the woman he loved—or believed he loved, anyway.

Which somehow would make everything worse. Because if Stephen said all the things he'd said and actually meant them at the time, then he wasn't mean or deceptive. He was merely inconstant.

And in that case, what was a declaration of love really worth? Not just Stephen's— anyone's. For the rest of her life, if Maude were ever to find herself listening again to the whispers of another lover, an expression of adoration and admiration, a fervent wish for a future together, she would have to wonder not *is this true?* but something far more slippery: *how long will this be true?* And then what could she possibly offer in return? *Be realistic.* Or, worse: *I love you too.*

"I blame myself," she said to Edith one night.

"That's always a helpful thing to do," Edith answered.

Maude smiled in the dark. They were lying in their cots in the tiny nurses' quarters at the end of the third floor. The blackout was still in effect, but since the end of the blitz, Maude and Edith had rediscovered the simple pleasure of sometimes lying awake on a summer night and talking to a friend. Usually Maude wouldn't bring up Stephen, out of courtesy for Edith. However angry Maude might be at Stephen, she knew that a lover's rejection couldn't compare to the loss that Edith had suffered. Still, a loss was what it was, and on this occasion Edith had encouraged her to talk about it.

"But the fact is I *am* to blame, to some extent," Maude was saying. "You weren't there, Edith. It's as if Stephen were trying to warn me, and I wouldn't listen. I told him I simply would have none of it, that I refused to even consider such a possibility."

"You can't seriously expect me to believe that Stephen was trying to warn you that in the end he would choose Helena over you. I mean, really, Maude. Helena was barely his wife. She refused to be good to him, she was barely civil to him, barely human. He wouldn't choose that over you."

"I don't know what I expect you to believe," Maude said. "I don't know what to believe myself." She sighed heavily. "No, you're right, of course. I suppose he wasn't trying to send me some sort of secret message. But he *was* encouraging me not to be some dopey schoolgirl, which is exactly what I turned out to be."

"It sounds to me like you were only wishing for a happy ending."

"I suppose I was," Maude said.

"But isn't that what we all want?" Edith asked.

"Yes, of course." Maude nodded. "But some of us are better at preparing ourselves for an unhappy ending than others."

"Some unhappy endings *no* amount of preparation—" Edith began softly, before breaking off.

"Oh, Edith. I wasn't thinking." Maude sat up in her cot and reached out to her friend in the dark, fumbling for her hand, clasping it between both her own hands. "I'm so sorry."

"Don't be." Edith squeezed Maude's hands back. "You have to talk about these things. You can't go around blaming yourself. Blame Stephen. Blame the war. War

changes people. Maybe something happened to change Stephen, and that's all
there is to it. But whatever the reason is,
it's nothing you did. Maybe one day after
the war, back at Oxford, you'll see
Stephen, and you can ask him then what
happened. Or not. The two of you can sit
and have a civil conversation over tea, or
you can nod hello and go your separate
ways. But whatever happens, Maude,
please promise me that you won't blame
yourself. Please, Maude. Promise me
that."

"All right," Maude said. She patted
Edith's hand, gave one last squeeze, and
let go. Then she slipped back onto her pillow. "I promise. Now, we'd better get some
sleep," she added, as she habitually did on
these occasions, "or we won't be any
good for anyone tomorrow."

Edith was right, up to a point. War did
change people. Not just in all the obvious
physical ways, the shortages and rationing
and sleeplessness and injuries and deaths.
But in other far more subtle ways. Edith,
for instance. How many times had Maude
observed her friend engaging in a routine
act of heroism that would have been

unimaginable only two years earlier? Maude would watch her at work and try to connect that memory of a younger, more innocent Edith, flirting outrageously with Ned at The Bear, with the actual Edith before her now, refusing to head down to the shelter with everyone else, staying on the third floor to be by the side of a delirious old woman with a head injury who couldn't be moved.

The war had changed Stephen too—of that much about Stephen, Maude could be sure. *How* it had changed him, though, was another matter entirely. What had happened to alter his attitude toward Maude? Had witnessing the fragility of life in combat somehow propelled him back toward Helena? Had his own brush with mortality, the piece of shrapnel that lodged in his leg, somehow helped him become more sympathetic to the emotional turmoil of his wife? Had he found on his return to Oxford that the two of them, each crippled in his or her own way, needed each other now more than ever? Or had the long absence simply awakened in him a new and somehow more profound appreciation for the comforts of home? Or was it something else entirely?

No. *Someone else.* On one of the hottest days that August, the heat collecting on the third floor of the hospital, the sweat slipping down the back of her uniform, this was the idea that came to Maude. But it didn't simply strike her, didn't merely over- take her. It arrived with such stark clarity that it actually chilled her. She shuddered so violently she nearly dropped the tray of medicine she was carrying down the hall- way. It was so obvious, once she'd thought it. How could she have missed it? Pre- cisely because it *was* so obvious—so un- mistakably right. It made so much sense Maude immediately knew it couldn't *not* be true. Her legs grew weak. Her hands were shaking. She had to prop herself against the wall, but that was no good. So she had to slip to the floor, and that was better. So she placed the tray there, closed her eyes, lowered her head, took deep breaths.

"Nurse Latham?"

Maude gazed up, glassily. Dr. Allen Drake was sprinting down the hallway to- ward her. It was cooler down here, near the tiles of the floor, she noticed. Cold, actually.

"I'm all right," she said. Her voice sounded slurred to her. Caked in ice.

"I'll be the judge. No, don't try to pick up the tray. Leave it there. Leave it there, I say. That medicine is too valuable for you to be juggling it around like that."

Maude tried to stand, felt flesh. A hand. His hand, Allen's hand, on her forehead.

"You're burning up."

"No," Maude said. "Freezing."

"Hush."

Other voices, other footsteps. Legs at eye level. Shoes whispering. Rubber soles. So soft, so quiet. So warm.

And then: nothing.

Nothing.

No war. No blackout. No blitz. No amputees or air raids, no shrapnel or sirens, no RAF visitors traveling in pairs to knock on doors, snap salutes, give away their news with one look into their eyes. No Stephen. No *no-Stephen,* either—no absence of Stephen, no note arriving out of the blue, no ache or emptiness or questions without answers.

No *nothing.*

Just sleep. A steep and spiraling and endless sleep, a swaddling sleep, a foundling's sleep. And then: something. A sound. A shadow. A voice and a figure. Two figures, talking. A man and a woman; a doctor and a nurse; Allen and Edith.

"I was dead," Maude heard herself say.

Allen and Edith stopped talking and turned to her.

"Ah, Nurse Latham," Allen said. "Welcome back to the world. We missed you."

"Oh, Maude," Edith said. "I'm so glad you're all right."

"I was dead," Maude said again, slowly.

"Hardly," Allen said. "Just a fever. A mean one, but still. It's a wonder more of us working on this side of the thermometer don't give out once in a while."

"But it was so dark," Maude said.

"I wouldn't be surprised," Allen said. "I gave you a little something, that's all."

"So empty," said Maude.

"Just a little something to help you sleep."

"And the war?" She opened her eyes and looked from Allen to Edith.

"What about the war?" said Allen. "It's

still on, if that's what you mean. Say, that must have been some dream. Well, don't go telling anyone or pretty soon everybody will want what I gave you."

"I wouldn't mind a little myself," Edith said, picking up Maude's hand from the side of the bed and giving it a squeeze.

"See what I mean?" Allen said. "I'll be back to check on you. I won't go far. Not that I could, even if I wanted," he added with a smile.

Maude tried to nod her head and return the smile, but already he was gone, striding down a long row of cots. Maude could see now that she herself was lying on a cot, in a far corner of the main ward on the third floor.

"He's pretty nice, once you get to know him," Edith said, pulling a stool close to Maude's cot.

"How long was I out?" Maude said.

"A full day," said Edith.

"But the others," Maude said, gesturing toward the other cots in the ward.

"We can manage fine without you for now," Edith said. "Here, I saved these for you," and she placed several newspapers on Maude's bedspread. They were folded open to the cryptic puzzles. "I've filled in a few of the answers, but feel free to solve away." She started to get up from the stool. "And Maude?"

Maude blinked at her.

"Do get your rest, or you'll be no good to anyone tomorrow."

And now Maude did manage to smile. And then she rested. She closed her eyes and waited for the emptiness or the darkness or the nothingness to swallow her again. But it didn't come. Her sleep this time was entirely unlike the fever dream. It was simply the same sleep as always: brittle, loud, and full of the war and Stephen.

And then the next morning she woke up and went back to work. The fever had passed, just as the fear that had accompanied the fainting spell eventually would pass. Not because she came to see the idea of Stephen with another woman—the nurse who tended to his injury in hospital, in Maude's most tortured fantasy—as unlikely. On the contrary, that idea never lost the clarity it achieved the very same moment it felled Maude in the hallway. Still, it passed, if only because it had to. Because in war there were only two choices: it passed, whatever "it" was; or it didn't. As long as bodies kept arriving at Brackett-on-Heath, Maude would have wounds to dress and nerves to soothe. And so: It passed.

She understood this fundamental truth now as she never had before in her life. This was the way in which the war had changed Maude. Edith was right about that—the war changed everyone. What Edith had been wrong about, though, was that Maude would have the opportunity to find out how the war had changed Stephen, once the fighting was over and their paths crossed at Oxford.

Maude would not be going back to Oxford, she'd decided. That period of her life was over now. It had been nice while it lasted, like childhood. And like childhood, when it was over, there was no going back. Sometimes, while on a break, Maude would drift outside the hospital, and if the weather weren't absolutely horrible, or the enemy were anywhere but directly over-head, the lawn that stretched all the way to the road into town was always filled with children. Some of the boys and girls were patients, those fortunate enough to be able to move about. And some of the boys and girls were the children of patients. But they were always out there, waving sticks and throwing stones and giving chase, as if there were no such thing as war, or at least as if they weren't in the middle of one. And then Maude would just stand there and close her eyes and raise her face to the sun and listen to their laughter.

"Ah, my favorite patient."

Maude turned to see Allen striding toward her across the gravel drive.

"I spotted you from a window up there," he went on, nodding his head back toward the hospital, "and I thought, What a brilliant idea, to get outside on this glorious day. Why couldn't I be clever enough to think of that?"

"I like to watch the children," Maude said, turning back to the field and shading her eyes.

"Yes, we could all take a lesson from them. Resilience and all that."

"Or innocence," Maude said. "Naïveté. Not knowing any better."

"Oh, I'm not so sure," said Allen. "I think they may know more than you think. Children always do, in my experience. Hear everything. Feel everything." He turned toward Maude. "What about you?"

"You mean, how naive am I?"

"Good lord, no." Allen adopted an expression that was somehow a smile but not a smile—an amused frown, perhaps. "I've no doubt you lost your innocence long ago, like all the rest of us, I'm afraid," he said. "No, I was referring to your experience with children."

"Oh." Maude was smiling now too. "I don't think I know much about children."

"Well, surely you were one once. A child, I mean. Where was that?"

"Oxford."

"What's that?"

She shook her head. "Never mind. A private joke, and not a very good one, at that." She turned toward Allen. "I'm sorry, but I should be getting back now."

"Of course." He looked away, squinting toward the field.

"But I've enjoyed our talk," Maude went on. "You know, I never did properly thank you for rescuing me the other day."

"Rescue? *You?* Hardly." Allen turned back to Maude. "You're probably the woman least in the need of rescue that I've ever met. Coming all the way over here from the States on your own. *Staying* over here. And then this business with the fellow in the Royal Navy who doesn't even have the decency—" He stopped himself.

"Oh," Maude said, after a moment. "So Edith told you." It was more a statement than a question.

"Well, yes, she did," Allen said somewhat sheepishly. "But only after I inquired." He offered his smile that wasn't a smile, then glanced away again, toward the children in the field. "I am sorry to hear about it, though. For your sake."

"Thank you."

"Look, Maude. The thing of it is, I'm afraid you and I might have gotten off on the wrong foot when you first came here, and I was wondering if by any chance you might care to, you know, one evening, the two of us—"

"Yes."

"What?" He turned to her. "Really? Well. Good. Excellent. Well. Well, then."

As surprised as Allen was by her response, Maude was even more so. Surprised, and pleased. It felt right, felt somehow *hopeful,* to say yes. Maybe it was the example of the children at play—their "re-silience," as Allen Drake had said—that in-spired her in that moment. But whatever it was, Maude found herself for the rest of the afternoon experiencing a sensation she realized she hadn't had since the start of the war: looking forward to something other than the end of the war.

She stood in her small room and gazed into its shallow closet. There, on the left side, were Edith's things, and on the right side were Maude's. The only vaguely fes-tive dresses she had with her here were three rather simple ones, and of these she chose the blue silk. And as for makeup, all she had left were a few little pots of it that she'd barely used since she'd come to the hospital. Nurses did not wear makeup. Now she stood before the small, tilted mir-ror and carefully traced the outline of her lips with a rather pale, doe-colored lipstick. She actually felt somewhat happy, she re-alized, preparing to go out for the evening, happy to be looking at herself in the mirror and not hating what she saw, happy to be preening and imagining sitting across the table from Allen.

At half-past six, Maude and Allen walked

across the lawn and down the road into town to have a drink at a pub called the Bantam, and an hour later they walked back to the hospital in the darkness of the blackout. They did the same the following evening. Then, on the third evening, they did it again.

"Is it my imagination, or is life becoming suspiciously normal?" Allen said on that occasion, during the walk back to the hospital. They were making their way across the lawn. The hospital loomed before them, as dark and hulking on a moonless night as if it were a ruin.

"I guess we're experiencing what they call a lull in the action," Maude said.

Maude glanced over at Allen, and even though he was right beside her, she couldn't make out his features in the dark. Still, she'd learned enough about his voice over the past few days so that she could tell he was smiling slightly, in that self-conscious way of his. What had they talked about in all that time while she was getting to learn the nuances of his voice? She couldn't say. The past two nights, when Maude had collapsed in her cot, Edith had begged for one morsel of her conversation with Allen, but Maude couldn't provide anything remotely delicious. She and Allen had talked about the hospital a little, and the war, of course, and Allen had mentioned that he was the son of a doctor in Dover, and Maude had reciprocated with the tale of the fabric manufacturer's daughter from Longwood Falls, New York. But it wasn't what they said to each other that Maude appreciated so much as that they said it at all. It was, Maude explained, simple companionship that Allen offered— that and something she didn't discuss with Edith: the not inconsiderable pleasure of sitting across from a good-looking man who is clearly taking pleasure in sitting across from you.

Maude and Allen now slowed their pace until they'd come to a full stop in the middle of the field. The hospital groundskeeper had cut the grass that afternoon, and the smell of the fresh-mown grass was intoxicating, Maude thought.

"I hate to go in," Allen said.

"Me too."

She felt Allen's hand on her shoulder, then along her arm, one finger raising gooseflesh.

"Oh, Maude. It's been wonderful to have someone to talk to these past few days."

"I feel the same way."

"You know, I'd love to take you away from here."

"Oh?"

"I was thinking perhaps we could go into London," he said with a trace of embarrassment and hesitation. "On a weekend. This weekend, even."

"Oh."

"Damn. I've said something wrong, haven't I?"

"No, it's nothing," Maude said. Then she said, "Really? You know my voice that well?"

"I hear it in my head all day long, even when you're not there," said Allen. "And then all night long. Look, I know London's not a terribly exotic destination. Or distant, for that matter. But it's probably as far as we can safely wander from the grounds of Brackett-on-Heath."

"Actually," Maude said, "London on a weekend sounds perfect."

She allowed herself to be kissed by Allen Drake. She allowed herself to kiss him back too, trying hard to summon up a sensation that would seem to indicate that the two of them might have a future.

In her previous trips to London, it had never once occurred to Maude to set foot inside the Savoy Hotel. Many times she'd passed it, walking from a day spent at the National Gallery to some West End theater at night, or meeting a friend for lunch along the Strand. But it had never occurred to her to actually go inside. Standing back from the road, fronted by doormen in ankle-length coats with brass buttons you could see even at that considerable distance, it hadn't seemed the kind of place you simply popped into unless you belonged there.

Which Maude now did. When she and Allen emerged from the Charing Cross railway station, she still had no idea where he was taking her. It was to be a surprise, he'd insisted. She had tried to tell him several times that she was too old for surprises, but he had responded that nobody was too old for surprises. And Maude had thought, I am, but she'd gone along with it anyway, because the desire to pleasantly surprise her had seemed so urgent to Allen.

And so she was walked up the Strand, and brought round a corner, and escorted along the walk past the Savoy Theatre, where the posters for the D'Oyly Carte holiday show were already hanging, and then through the gleaming golden entrance of the hotel. Allen gave his name at the desk, and a moment later a bellman appeared at their side to relieve them of their luggage and lead them to their room.

Their room, Maude thought at once, seemed oddly familiar, and after a moment she realized where she'd encountered it before: the movies. It was, she thought, every hotel suite she'd ever seen on the screen. It had a sitting room, a bedroom, a powder room, and a piano—a grand piano, white and shining. Minutes later, thanks to Allen's advance planning, their suite also had a complete dinner for two, carted in by two bellmen and served to Maude and Allen on a table that seemed to appear out of nowhere. The tablecloth was linen, the flatware china, the utensils silver. The soup was oxtail, the main course duck à l'orange, the dessert a delicious trifle, soaked in sweet wine and studded with nuts and berries. For the coffee, there was cream. To one side, a champagne bucket sweated.

"There *is* a war on," Maude said, "isn't there?"

"Not tonight," Allen answered. "Not this weekend."

Maude didn't know what else to say. She circled the table while Allen saw the servants out. Then she circulated throughout the entire suite, an expedition that took several minutes. When Allen reappeared she looked up from the keyboard in the corner and said, "Do you even play the piano?"

She'd gone too far. She saw that at once. Allen's prideful expression—his keen anticipation of her response—collapsed utterly. At once he began explaining that the wife of the hotel's manager had been a patient under his care at Brackett-on-Heath a year earlier, and that these amenities were nothing compared to what military brass and gangsters and royalty could command on a moment's notice, and that he thought that they—the two of them, Allen and Maude—deserved the best, and he was sorry if he was mistaken.

For her part, Maude shook her head and explained that it was just *such* a surprise—so overwhelming and out of the blue—she didn't know what to say, but that she knew he was absolutely right: a surprise like this is just what she needed. It would indeed be a memorable evening, she said—a memorable weekend. Let's make it memorable, she told him.

And a grateful Allen visibly relaxed, and smiled, and said, *Let's.*

Maude had had no regrets about leaving home and crossing the ocean at a difficult time in the history of the world. She'd even had no regrets about staying on in England, despite her parents' pleas, Stephen's words of caution, and then his betrayal. Edith had been right about this too: You could blame the war, but not yourself. Maude had made the best choices she could have made at the time, based on the information she had then and, more to the point, who she was then: a young woman with certain romantic notions about how to live in the world.

But she was not that woman anymore. The time had come—had long since passed, in fact—for her to be realistic. The love that Maude expected to have with Allen was not the love she'd once wanted from Stephen. But it would be real, and it would be enough, she decided, for the duration.

CHAPTER SEVEN

It was strange the way a life that did not feel natural could still somehow feel routine. So it was with a country in the middle of a war. The rules, the rationing, the losses, the fear: all of it became, somehow, par for the course. And so it was, also, for Maude Latham and Allen Drake. She hadn't grown to find passion with him over time exactly, as he'd suggested she might, and yet she'd accepted their ongoing love relationship as something that *fit* into her life. She let it fit there; she kept it going, even though she never once thought to herself, *he is the one.* That was a feeling that usually only comes once in someone's life, and even then, only if she's lucky.

So Maude was lucky, perhaps. Lucky to have had what she'd once had with

Stephen; lucky to be alive, lucky to be de-
voting her life to something worthwhile and
necessary. She really couldn't complain.
This, anyway, was what she thought when
she wrote home to her parents in 1941, explaining to them about Allen and glancingly
mentioning Stephen, though not by name.
Her parents wrote back immediately, telling
her they were pleased she had met someone she cared for and hoped that her "relationship with this Dr. Drake" could help
take her mind off the difficulties and chal-
lenges of her life. Which was, of course, an
impossibility. The war had informed her
life; it *was* her life.

And then, the next thing she knew, her
parents' lives were changed as well, for at
the very end of the year the United States
was in the war too. The entire world had
gone mad; didn't everyone see that? Blood
was spreading out all over the jagged continent of Europe, and now into the Pacific
as well. Her parents suddenly found themselves with parts to play in the drama, and
no more was said about the rather tire-
some, melodramatic love life of their way-
ward British daughter.

Maude's mother went to work for the

American Red Cross, packing boxes of medical supplies to send overseas. And her father's factories were now manufacturing bandages instead of fabric for dresses. Maude's sister, Ruthie, had learned to knit and was making scarves "for our boys," as she proudly put it in a letter. How easy it was to feel ownership in wartime, Maude thought. When Stephen had first gone off to join the Royal Navy two years earlier, she'd thought of him as *hers*. Was that simply a proprietary delusion inspired by war? She had no way of knowing anymore. He'd never been hers, not really; he'd always been his wife's, and whatever woman had replaced Maude in his affections.

Maude kept in contact with her parents as best she could over the months, the years, hearing all sorts of stories of American tragedy and heroism, including one about her sweet cousin Henry from Ohio, who had joined the Marines and been immediately killed at Guadalcanal. The tragedies continued with no abatement, yet there were victories too, more of them, the Germans on the defensive, and slowly, slowly, the war began to turn. It took time, years of time; and fresh soldiers were constantly needed to replenish the ones who hadn't made it. Still they went, these men, these *boys,* some of them, doing what was required of them, just as Maude had done what was needed when she showed up that morning in September of 1939 and told the head of hospital personnel she was there to help.

It still amazed her the way a war could transform lives, not just through death, but also through experience. The day that Maude first appeared at the hospital, she'd been dewy and innocent and in some ways ridiculous. Ridiculously optimistic. That had been stripped away, bit by bit, by all the things she'd seen: the personal suffering of the patients she cared for, and also the rude awakening she'd been given about the vagaries of love. The hopefulness Maude had once felt, and the sustenance that was provided by the promise of eventually being united forever with Stephen, was long gone, of course, leaving behind a wary, cool customer. She was a woman who had seen it all and who was now surprised by nothing.

She'd grown older; they all had. War had

changed the shape of everything, even her sense of time. Time was sneaky and deceptive, inching on as though it was unaware of the ravages of war. Time was impervious. By 1944, Maude at age twenty-four was the chief nurse on the trauma unit, a skilled and seasoned practitioner who kept her head in times of trouble. She seemed decades older and infinitely more serious than she'd once been. She was no longer the ingenue but instead, if life itself were a play, she would have been cast as the knowing, slightly embittered woman who has been dealt a blow at the end of the first act. Maude was still hauntingly pretty, yet slightly drawn. She was a woman who had seen too much to ever be innocent again, or to ever fully be happy again, she suspected, even with the promise of victory lurking somewhere in the not-too-distant future.

One night in June, shortly after the surge and excitement of D-day, Maude and Allen went out for the evening to the local pub called the Bantam that they sometimes visited. The place was lively and filled with talk; someone, somewhere, was singing, and a loud hooting was coming from a table of elderly men, one of whom had just told a joke. How different the atmosphere was, Maude thought, from the Rose and Stag. Though, of course, she hadn't been there since right before the war started. Certainly back then every pub in England had been quiet and somber with worry. People had drunk their pints quickly, longing for the effects of the alcohol to wash across them and lightly anesthetize them from what was about to come. But now, here in the undistinguished Bantam, people were enjoying themselves. Allen was one of the ones enjoying himself, she realized, looking at his relaxed face and the way he stretched out in his chair, making jokes with the barman and a customer across the way whom he recognized. Maude, however, wasn't having a very good time. This place was just a pub; it would never be "their" place, hers and Allen's, try as he might to make that so.

But she enjoyed being with him wherever they went. They never ran out of topics to discuss, and he was always full of interesting stories from the operating theater, or from his medical training, or from something he'd read in a journal and wanted to pass along to Maude. She also knew him to be an excellent physician, not only technically but also in terms of his compassion, which he possessed in great quantity, unlike some of the other doctors at the hospital.

He was a good person; that was indisputable, and she loved him for that reason and others. Allen Drake was an attractive man in all ways, and they'd developed a rhythm together, as all couples do over time. The first time he'd told her he loved her, she'd easily and honestly said, "I love you too," and for the rest of the evening a golden glow had wrapped itself around the two of them. It was the very particular glow that existed whenever love was admitted and then reciprocated.

But love came in various varieties, Maude knew. The way Allen loved her was in all likelihood different from the way she loved him. And both were different from the way that Maude had loved Stephen. Not to mention the way she'd thought Stephen had loved her too.

But this, now, with Allen; it still counted as love. He could make her feel cherished and special; he could make her cry out in pleasure whenever they made love. So she let herself be one half of a couple, going out for drinks with him and letting him take her to dinner, and truly being appreciative when he bought her small gifts: a simple brooch, an ornament for her hair in the shape of a bird.

But now, over pints of ale in the noisy, warm bar, Allen wanted to talk about their plans "for after," as he delicately put it.

"I can't even imagine an after," said Maude.

"But there will be one," he said, smiling a little. "And we'll have to start from scratch. All of us will, not just here in England but everywhere in Europe. It will take decades, I think, just even to return to a life that remotely resembles the one that was there before."

"Oh yes," Maude said softly, "I imagine you're right."

In a way, she realized that the war had protected her from putting together a life that didn't include Stephen. It had kept her busy in a time that otherwise might have been fueled by self-pity. She felt vaguely panicked at the idea that one of these days she would have to create a life for herself that included more than round-the-clock patient care and exhaustion and dinners out with Allen Drake. He didn't want to pressure her, he said, but clearly he was eager to assemble a life for himself—for both of them—after the war.

"I think it's time to start thinking about all that, Maude," he said. "At least, it's time to start having a conversation or two about it. Nothing definitive, only something preliminary. You don't need to sign on the dotted line."

"I know," she said, but she wasn't happy with this conversation. It had taken her by surprise, and she didn't know what to say. "Look, darling—" she began, but Allen interrupted.

"Don't call me that," he said quietly, "unless you mean it."

"I do mean it."

"Oh, I suppose you do," said Allen, "or at least you think you do. Because you feel tenderly toward me, is that it?"

"Well, yes, it's part of it," Maude said.

"Maude, I want more than anything in the world to be considered your darling," he said, "but saying it doesn't make it so."

"I don't understand," Maude said.

"Look," he said, "you seem taken aback by the idea of spending the rest of your life with me. It's almost as though you've never really taken the idea seriously."

"I have so," Maude tried.

"Perhaps," said Allen, "but the war was always conveniently in the way, wasn't it? The war always allowed you to put off figuring out how you wanted to spend the rest of your life."

Maude nodded. "Please don't hate me for it," she said.

"How could I ever hate you?" Allen said. "I love you. You're the most wonderful woman I've ever known. I admire you more than you know. God, Maude, I think I even worship you."

"That's never a very good idea," Maude said quietly. "Worship, I think, is best reserved for God, not for a woman you happen to fancy."

"No, I suppose you're right," said Allen. "But I think of you all the time, and whenever I do, it just feels . . . well, wonderful." Tears came to him then, and he squeezed his eyes shut, turning away from her.

"Oh, Allen," Maude said. "I hate to see

you so unhappy. Isn't there anything I can do?"

He was quiet for a while and then he turned back to her, his eyes bright. Slowly, Allen Drake shook his head. "No," he said simply, "I don't think there is. You've always been completely honest with me, that's always been something I could count on. From the start you told me where you stood. You never lied. I do believe you love me in the best way you can." He paused, took a deep drink from his glass, then set it down. "But I guess I also see now, for the first time, since things are starting to wind down in Europe, that I need a little more than that."

"Oh," was all Maude could say in a small voice. "I see."

Allen took a drink of his ale. The entire next table suddenly broke out into howling laughter at something that one of them had said. Amid the laughter, and the general gaiety, Maude and Allen were set in relief by their unhappiness.

Maude took Allen's hand. There was a callus there on the back of the thumb, and she stroked it gently. These hands had been doing so much work for years; Allen

was a first-rate surgeon. He was also a
tender lover, never awkward or false. They
had been as true to each other as each of
them was capable of being. There was
nothing more that anyone could do for
each other in the world, Maude thought.
You did the best you could, you bumped
along, you tried, and if, in the end, your
best wasn't good enough, well, so be it.

Her best wasn't good enough. Maude
finished her drink, barely feeling the cold
ale go down her throat. Allen was breaking
off their relationship, doing it in person, unlike Stephen, who had done it in a letter—
no, not even in a letter, but in a poem that
someone else had written. *I am the kind of
woman whom men break away from,* she
thought to herself as she sat in that dark,
noisy pub and briefly wondered what it
was about her that was apparently so in-
adequate when it came to the task of love.

They actually stayed friends, which was
the only consolation Maude felt after Allen
told her they ought not see each other anymore. "We can stay friends, you know,"
he'd said at the time, and though Maude
asked him how often he imagined ex-

lovers said such a thing to each other and how often it turned out to be possible, in their case it really was possible. When she'd had a particularly difficult day at the hospital and was collapsed in a chair in the staff lounge or the dining room, he'd sometimes come and sit beside her and they'd talk for a while, and she'd feel better. It was too bad, Maude thought, that what she wanted in a man apparently wasn't primarily comfort and strength. Because Allen had both of these qualities in spades; most women would find him more than suitable.

She was the one who wasn't suitable. That was what she'd come to realize.

Then one afternoon that June Maude found herself tending to the latest group of soldiers that had arrived in Brackett-on-Heath for assessment and treatment. Walking up and down the ward, stopping to take a pulse here and have a brief chat there, she walked past a bed, and then something made her stop. The man lying in the bed looked familiar, though she couldn't quite place him. He had short blond hair like a shorn lamb, and his features were slightly sharp and bright. He was looking at her too, and his face was serious, inquisitive.

Maude lifted the chart clipped to the iron footrail of his bed and saw his name. "Lieutenant Jared Thomson," she read, and then it all came back to her: the first time he had come to the hospital, bearing a letter from Stephen. He'd been smiling then, even though the letter he handed her contained within it news that would crush her. He had been Stephen's messenger; what did he know? Perhaps very little.

And now here he was again, though this time he wasn't smiling. He was here to be treated for shock, according to his chart. "Hello," she said, approaching the side of the bed.

"Nurse . . . Latham, is it?" said Thomson. "Do you remember me?"

"Yes," said Maude, "I do. Though I see that you're here for very different reasons this time."

"Yes," he said. "I should say so."

Maude pulled up a chair and sat down. "Tell me what's been happening to you," she said.

"Oh," said the young man, "it's not really

such a big deal. In fact, I don't even think I need to be here."

"Lieutenant Thomson," Maude said gently, "if you didn't need to be here, then I'm sure you wouldn't be."

"I'm not as bad as some," he said, but as he reached onto his bedside table to pick up the glass of water that sat there, she saw how severely his hand was shaking. Shock could do that, Maude knew; she'd seen men try to light cigarettes and end up waving a lit match around in the air as though it were a wand. Though the initial sight of him had made her stiffen, thinking of the letter, she was of course sympathetic to him as well and wanted to help, for it was her job.

"How long have the tremors been with you?" she asked, steadying the glass as he drank from it.

"The tremors," he said when he was done drinking. "Is that what that is? And here I've been thinking it was just the ground shaking from another explosive."

Maude smiled. "In a way," she said, "it is related to the ground shaking. Your whole nervous system has been rocked to its core. Soldiers don't realize the extent of the stress that constant explosions can cause, but believe me, we take it very seriously here."

"And what's the cure?" the lieutenant asked.

"Well, there is no actual cure, exactly," said Maude. "But we'll treat you with a combination of rest and sedatives and perhaps some hydrotherapy—"

"What's that?" he asked.

"Baths," Maude said. "Just a fancy name for baths."

"Ah," he said, and he was smiling now too.

"We'll take good care of you," Maude promised. "We've seen plenty of patients like yourself."

"Thank you," Lieutenant Thomson said. "I guess I do need to be here. My hands sometimes don't obey me the way I want them to."

"How about your legs?" she asked.

"Those too," he admitted. "I've fallen down once or twice."

"And sleep?" Maude wanted to know. "Are you able to have a comfortable night?"

"Sometimes," Lieutenant Thomson said.

But his first night at Brackett-on-Heath wasn't one of those times. At 2 A.M. when Maude was carrying a battery-run torch and making a final tour of the wards before retiring for the night, she heard cries and moans coming from one of the beds, and then she realized it was he. She strode over, and he was thrashing around in his bed, in the throes of a nightmare. His face was contorted, as if in pain, and he was muttering aloud. "No, look, don't go over there," he was saying. "Baker, Forrest, go tell Kendall. Quick, quick."

Maude froze; he'd said "Kendall." It was unmistakable. So Lieutenant Thomson had probably still been stationed with Stephen very recently; unless, of course, he was remembering something that had happened a while ago. Most likely, she thought, he still knew Stephen. She felt *herself* tremble, like someone in shock. But she put her emotions aside and gently shook the young man awake. "It's all right, Lieutenant Thomson," she said gently. "You were dreaming. Everything is fine. You're not in danger."

Lieutenant Thomson blinked rapidly and

looked around. "What is this place?" he asked anxiously.

"Brackett-on-Heath Hospital, just outside London," Maude told him. "You're a patient here, but you're going to be fine."

"Oh," he said, getting his bearings and looking around the ward in the darkness. The beam from Maude's torch lit both their faces with an eerie glow, as if they were meeting now in the underworld. "Sorry to cause all this fuss," he said.

"Don't apologize," said Maude, and she helped him drink some water and pulled up a chair beside his bed again. It was true that Maude sometimes sat and visited with a patient, but she knew that what drew her to this particular patient was something more complex than a nurse's compassion.

She was intensely curious about Stephen, and yet she didn't want to exhibit it; instead, she wanted to seem anything but curious. But she *was* curious, that was the thing she realized. Though she'd told herself she was well beyond Stephen—and that had to be true, certainly—being confronted by the sight of Stephen's colleague and friend brought him to life once again, unbidden. She wanted to know about him all of a sudden, after steeling herself to the facts of the situation since the day Jared Thomson had arrived with that letter. Who knew if he was even alive? It had been years ago; anything could have happened by now.

The ward was quiet tonight; distantly a patient moaned, and another one was insistently calling out for something to drink, but a nurse attended to him, striding down the center of the ward with a fresh pitcher of ice water. Maude and the lieutenant sat together for a little while. Then, in a voice that she hoped seemed detached, she said, "You know, during your nightmare you shouted out the name 'Kendall.' "

"Did I?" said Lieutenant Thomson. "How curious."

"I assume," said Maude, "that that referred to my old friend Commander Kendall."

"Suppose so," he said.

"How is my old friend Commander Kendall?" asked Maude. "Are you still in contact with him?"

Lieutenant Thomson regarded her. "You know I'm not allowed to reveal any information like that," he said. "It's classified."

"Of course," Maude said quickly. "I'd forgotten," though she realized that his answer must mean that in fact he was still stationed with Stephen. Stephen was alive. He was still in the war, and Lieutenant Jared Thomson still knew him well. Her heart skipped a little.

"Sorry," Lieutenant Thomson said.

"Not at all," said Maude. Then she stood. "Well," she said, "I should be turning in for the night. And so should you. Shall I give you a sedative, Lieutenant?"

"No, thank you just the same. I'd rather go it alone, if you don't mind," he said. "And please, won't you call me Jared?"

"All right then. Good night, Jared," she said, and then she walked back through the darkened ward, though she wondered how in the world she would sleep tonight.

Over the next few days, Maude found herself spending a fair amount of time with Jared Thomson. Because she was head of the unit, she could delegate responsibility for the different patients, keeping some of them under her own wing, and he was one of the ones she chose for herself. His was a much less severe case of shock than some of the others, who could barely speak or function on their own, and so she allowed him a great deal of freedom to walk around the hospital, thinking it would do him some good to be up and about. She even sent him on a few simple errands, letting him push the library cart up to the pediatric ward, or asking him to cut fresh flowers from the hospital's small garden to decorate some of the different wards. And as the days passed he improved considerably. There was a greater spring to his step, and his eyes had less of a frightened quality to them. He seemed to be relaxing here at the hospital, as he was supposed to do.

"You're feeling better, I see," she said once when she came upon him in the patients' sunroom, where he was sitting in a wicker chair, his head tilted back into the sunlight that streamed through the window.

"Oh yes, thanks, I am," he said.

"I imagine you'll be discharged rather soon," she said.

"Oh, really? That's great," he said. "You've been very helpful to me," he went on. "It means so much to have someone asking after one's health and one's welfare. It makes all the difference."

"Yes, I would imagine so," Maude replied.

"I've heard that you're a particularly caring individual," he went on, which seemed to be a slightly surprising remark, though she didn't comment on that.

"Thank you," she said. "But if the patients feel I'm very caring, then it's just because I'm doing my job."

"Not just the patients," Jared said lightly.

"What's that?" Maude asked.

"Oh, nothing," he said with a slight smile.

"No, really, tell me what you meant," said Maude.

"I just meant," he went on, "that I've heard from other quarters that you're very kind."

"Other quarters," said Maude drolly. "I see."

And then she was summoned by one of the doctors and had to go off and take care of another patient.

At dinner that night with Edith and Allen in the staff dining room, he lightly asked her if everything was all right.

"Perfectly," said Maude. "Why?"

"Oh, you seem to be somewhere else," he commented.

"Absolutely," said Edith. "I've been trying to have a decent conversation with you for days, Maude."

"I'm sorry," Maude said. "There's just so much work, that's all."

But she knew they were right; she was distracted, for the reappearance of Jared Thomson had unexpectedly shuttled her back to Oxford and her days as a student who was in love with her tutor. Those days were irretrievable, though, and the girl she'd been then was gone too, not to mention the man she'd loved. Who knew what Stephen was even like anymore?

Jared Thomson knew. But he wasn't telling.

Sometimes it seemed to be a game of sorts, in which Jared possessed information that Maude wanted, and the more he withheld it from her, the more she wanted it. It was as though she'd been able to keep her truest feelings for Stephen on a so-called back burner during the years since she'd received that letter, yet suddenly, with Jared here in hospital, everything had come rushing forward again: all the love she'd once felt, and the intensity of the anguish at losing that love. It doesn't just *end,* she realized. A love like that goes on and on, regardless of the particulars of circumstance.

And then one day, the day before he was to be discharged from the hospital, Jared Thomson approached Maude while she was sitting at the nurses' station with the day's crossword puzzle open in front of her, and a pen poised in the air above the grid.

"Ah, I see you're doing the cryptic puzzle," he said.

"They relax me," Maude admitted.

"Yes, I've heard they can be most restful now and then," he said.

She looked at him, took note of his neutral smile, yet was also aware of a kind of playfulness beneath the words—a peculiar tone that had been present once in a while since he'd arrived.

"Yes," Maude said. "They're one of my favorite distractions."

"I thought as much," said Jared. "In fact, I was rather hoping you'd say something like that."

"Why?" she asked him, confused. "Why were you hoping I did?"

"Oh, because I remember that when I came here the first time, you were solving one."

"That's right," Maude said, suddenly remembering that she'd been filling in a crossword puzzle the day that Jared showed up with Stephen's letter.

"Men in the British military enjoy crossword puzzles too, you know."

"Oh," said Maude, still not understanding where this was going. "You mean, *you* do?"

"Oh no, not me personally," said Jared. "Me, I'm rather an oaf when it comes to word games. You should see me at anagrams. A right dud, I am. No, I was never one for puzzles, though some of the other naval men are extremely clever at puzzles."

This was becoming more peculiar with every passing moment. If he was trying to hint to her that Stephen liked solving cryptic puzzles, well, that was all well and good, though she'd never known him to pick up a puzzle in his life. "I see," Maude said faintly, though her interest was sharpening further.

"That's the *Times* you've got there, yes?" said Jared, and Maude nodded.

"Yes," she said. "I get it every day."

"Ah," he said.

"Do you disapprove?" Maude asked.

"Oh no, not at all," said Jared. "It's just . . . oh, nothing."

"Tell me," said Maude.

"Oh, it's just that I've been told that the puzzles in the *Independent* are much better."

"I never heard that."

"Oh, it's true," he said. "The solutions are far more satisfying."

"Well," said Maude, feeling slightly annoyed at this conversation, "I actually prefer the *Times.*"

"No, no," he said insistently. "You really ought to switch to the *Independent.*"

"I'll give it some thought," she said.

"I'm leaving hospital tomorrow," he said. "But after I do, I hope you'll think about my suggestion. As I said, I think a woman like you will find it much more to your liking."

Then Maude was summoned to the room of a patient, so she didn't have a chance to say to Jared: Just what are you doing? Why are you behaving in such a perverse manner? Why would he care which newspaper's crossword puzzle she solved every day?

And then, the next morning, after he'd been discharged and she was bending over to find a vein in a new patient's arm, the answer suddenly arrived, out of no-where.

She'd been an idiot, resisting what he wanted her to know about the *Independent* versus the *Times.* The *Independent*'s crossword puzzle would definitely be more to her liking, he'd insisted. And why was that?

Because there would be a message for her in it.

And why would Lieutenant Jared Thomson need to send her a message in a cryptic crossword puzzle?

Well, he wouldn't. Because the message wouldn't be from him. It would be from someone else. From Stephen, of course. And he would be encrypting it like this, rather than letting Jared relay Stephen's thoughts in person, because he wouldn't want Jared to know whatever message he had for Maude. His message would be private.

Which begged the question: Why would Stephen Kendall want to send a private message to Maude? What would he have to say to her after all this time that was such a secret? What, in fact, would he have to say to her at all? It had been four years since she'd received that awful, cold letter from him. If he thought he could simply waltz back into her life, he was mistaken. If he wanted to say "I made a mistake," then she wouldn't let him back in. That "mistake" of his had caused her immense suffering. She'd been so lonely throughout the war—even when she was with Allen. If only he'd still been waiting for her back then—If only he'd kept his promise, as he'd sworn he would—then the separation from him wouldn't have been as difficult. She could have withstood it, the way thousands of women withstood the separation from their lovers or husbands during wartime.

But he'd discarded her, told her he no longer loved her. He'd been like the stag in the dream, leaping away carelessly, leaving her to fend for herself. And if he wanted to come back, after all this time, she'd have to say no.

But still, her curiosity had been aroused, if nothing else. He had a message to send her, and he was still in the navy and couldn't get it to her any way but this way. She would receive it, whatever it was.

"Oh, here's half of the *Times,*" Edith said the following morning, handing Maude part of the newspaper at breakfast, as she often did. Edith kept news and fashion first, giving Maude the crossword and the book page, and then later on, the women switched.

"Thanks, but not today," Maude said. She stood up and drifted across the small dining room to a table where a few nurses sat together. The *Independent* lay in scattered sections across the table. There, lying unattended, its grid empty, was the cryptic puzzle.

"Hello, Maude, want to join us?" a nurse named Constance asked. "We're discussing something vital to our country's national security."

"Indeed," said one of the others. "The topic is whether or not Cary Grant is sexier than Clark Gable."

"Clark Gable," announced Constance,

"has ears like the handles of a Grecian urn."

"Oh, I'm afraid this topic is far too lofty for me," said Maude.

"Nonsense," said one of the other women. "With your Oxford education, you could teach us all a few things."

"Not today, anyway," said Maude with a smile. Then casually she asked, "Mind if I steal your crossword?"

"Oh, do take it," said Constance. "I haven't the energy to devote to these things anymore."

So Maude took the crossword puzzle and left the dining room. She went straight to her room, sat down on the cot, and systematically began to fill in the answers. It wasn't all that difficult, this puzzle; in fact, it was slightly easier to solve than the puzzle in the *Times.* But nothing jumped out at her or seemed remotely messagelike. She didn't have a chance to finish the puzzle before work hours but put it aside, hoping to do so later. At the end of the day, after she'd gotten all the answers (with a little help from Dr. Manning, who'd first instructed her on the art of solving cryptics), she stared helplessly at the filled-in grid. Nothing. Nothing from Stephen.

The next day she tried the puzzle again, and the next, but still nothing struck her as being significant. And then, the following morning, as she dutifully filled in the answers, she came upon this clue, which happened to be 14 across: "Stood for a flower." And the answer, she quickly realized, was *rose. Rose* was a flower, and it also meant "stood." It was a common word, and might have been there coincidentally, but somehow she didn't think so.

The following morning, after snatching the puzzle away from a group of young doctors in the dining room, Maude found that the clue for 14 across was: "St. Agnes shelters male animal." This was a so-called hidden answer. The first four letters of "St. Agnes" spelled out "stag," which was, of course, a male animal.

Maude felt herself shiver. It was as though a mystery were unfolding before her, only she had no idea of its purpose. What would all of this lead to? If Stephen just wanted to say hello to Maude after all this time through a series of clever crossword clues, then the game would soon grow tedious.

But he'd never been a frivolous person, and why, after years spent in the war, would he suddenly become one? It really didn't make any sense to her at all, and there was no one to ask about it.

The next morning, the puzzle in the *Independent* revealed the extent of his seriousness: "Root worm turns in a day," read the clue to 14 across, and it didn't take very long for Maude, by now an old hand at cryptic puzzles, to rearrange the letters in *root worm* so that they spelled out a word that just might have significance:

Tomorrow.

CHAPTER EIGHT

Tomorrow.

Saturday.

The newspaper trembling in her hand, Maude returned to her living quarters and placed the puzzle gently on her cot. Then she retrieved the previous two days' puzzles from her nightstand drawer and laid out the entire set, side by side. There they were, a trio of individual clues, seemingly unremarkable, each meaningless on its own. *Rose. Stag. Tomorrow.* Put them together, though, and suddenly they acquired a new meaning, but only if you knew what to look for. Only if this particular combination of words carried a special set of associations for you.

Only, that is, if you were Maude Latham.

She was being summoned. Across the

years and from some secret wartime location Stephen was calling out to her. Jared
Thomson clearly must have returned to
wherever it was he and Stephen were stationed. And their duties clearly must have
something to do with naval intelligence, if
they could command the cryptic puzzle in
a newspaper for the purpose of sending
messages. They probably had an operative
on staff at the *Independent,* which was
why Jared had been so keen for Maude to
consult that newspaper rather than the
Times. Very possibly they'd been using the
newspaper and its puzzle to send messages throughout the war. All Jared had to
do, upon his return, was tell Stephen that
he knew a way to contact Maude Latham,
if he so desired. And Stephen apparently
did.

But why?

"I just don't understand," Maude said
that evening, displaying the three puzzles
for Edith's benefit and explaining the series
of mysterious conversations she'd been
having with Jared Thomson.

"What's to understand?" said Edith.
"The message seems pretty clear to me. I
wouldn't have believed it unless I'd seen it

with my own eyes, but there it is. In black and white, so to speak."

"No, I understand the *message,*" Maude said. "Or I guess I do anyway, because what else can it mean but that I should go to the Rose and Stag tomorrow? What I don't understand is why. Why would Stephen want to see me after all these years?"

"An excellent question, Maude," said Edith. "And as I'm sure you know, there's only one way to find out."

Edith was right, as usual—both that there was only one way to find out, and that Maude already knew it. Maude would have to do as she'd been told. How could she possibly refuse an opportunity so rife with intrigue? She simply had no choice.

Or did she? That night Maude lay awake in her cot for a long time, turning over endlessly all the possible motives that Stephen might have for wanting to see her again. Clearly he had something to tell her—but about what? Them—the two of them, Maude and Stephen? There *was* no Maude and Stephen, not anymore, and not for the longest time. There was Maude; there was Stephen; and that was that. There was

Maude and *Allen,* of course—or, at any rate, there *had* been Maude and Allen. And there was Stephen and Helena—or, perhaps, had been.

Maybe that was what he wanted to see Maude about, if indeed the meaning of the message was that Stephen would be meeting her at the Rose and Stag tomorrow. Maybe he wanted to tell her something about Helena.

She'd died. She'd finally expired of some side effect of the acute sensitivity that had been plaguing her and Stephen for years. Or somehow Helena had been killed in the war—though Maude couldn't recall hearing of any bombing runs over Oxford *or* Devon, where she'd lived for a while with her family. On the other hand, Helena might still be very much alive but "dead" to Stephen, in a manner of speaking. Maybe he'd finally worked up the courage to leave her after all, and this was the news he wanted to tell Maude. Or maybe Helena had left *him.* Either way, it was entirely possible that the entire elaborate code that had been playing itself out over the past few days in the pages of the

Independent was a way for Stephen to win Maude back.

Maude, however, was no longer winnable—not by Stephen, at any rate, not any longer. But Stephen couldn't know that, and he might well be proceeding under the assumption that he could somehow undo what he'd done to her—to them—years earlier. Maude turned on her side and made a mental note to choose only the plainest attire for her trip into London the following morning—a simple skirt and blouse, and sensible shoes. The last thing she wanted was to give Stephen a wrong impression, that she felt the need to appear attractive for his sake. Because the fact was, she *didn't* feel the need. Once, Stephen Kendall had found her desirable. Since then, Allen Drake had found her desirable. Maude had no reason to doubt that in the months and years to come other men would find her equally desirable. She didn't need to prove anything to Stephen, and she didn't need to prove anything to herself.

Of course, Maude thought, turning to her other side, it was also possible that Stephen wanted to see Maude not to reconcile, but only in order to apologize. To explain his callous behavior. Maybe all he wanted, after all this time, was to ask her forgiveness. Maybe the guilt of how he'd handled their separation had haunted him throughout the war until finally he could bear it no more. *I was a cad,* Maude imagined him blurting in one especially melodramatic yet satisfying fantasy. *You deserved better from me.* To which she would respond, crisply, with the kind of supreme indifference that might make the royal family proud, *I know.*

The war, she thought. The war was the wild card in all these considerations. Had it taken Stephen so long to get in touch with her because he'd been *unable* to contact her during the war? Had he in fact wanted to tell her in person all along but couldn't, so he'd resorted instead to writing her a note and forwarding it through an emissary? Or had he taken so long simply because of *who he was*—because of the defects in his character? Had he recognized belatedly the cowardice in writing her a note, but couldn't own up to his poor judgment until it was convenient for him—until either the guilt was too great or he'd changed his mind and wanted her back?

More to the point: Did it matter? Did Maude really care which obstacle he'd had to overcome—the war, or his own limitations?

The following morning, Maude awoke early, walked down the third-floor hallway to the other end of the building, and checked the clipboard hanging on the wall outside the operating theater. She saw that an emergency surgery, an appendectomy for a patient who had been hospitalized for an eye wound, had been added to the schedule for 7 A.M.

Perfect.

Maude signed the nurses' registry, entered the scrub room, and donned a surgical outfit. Two other nurses were there already, and the three of them made small talk while they washed their hands. Over the past five years, Maude had been through this procedure hundreds of times—no, thousands of times, easily. She knew what pleasantry to exchange with which nurse, what instruments to lay out in the operating room for which type of surgery, and the professional needs of each surgeon on the premises—in this case, a Dr. Percy, or "Dr. Perspiration," as the nurses referred to him behind his back, after his propensity for generating a notable quantity of sweat, which required the nurses who assisted in his operations to stock an extra supply of white cloths specifically for the purpose of wiping his forehead. Then the three nurses backed their way through the swinging doors that led into the operating room and got to work. In each detail the operation for which Maude had volunteered at the last minute this Saturday morning was no different from any other surgery she had attended over the past five years, and far more routine than most, except for the fact that her motive was more than purely medical: it would help distract her from the thought of Stephen sitting in the pub of the Rose and Stag, or worse, in their old room there, waiting for the arrival of the old lover who would never appear.

"Maude."

She looked up. The surgery was well under way now; the patient lay open on the operating table before the doctor and three attending nurses. But a fourth nurse had entered the room and spoken a single word, and Maude could see in the narrow eyes above the surgical mask that it was Edith.

"What is it, Nurse Waterstone?" Dr. Percy snapped. "We're quite busy here, or haven't you noticed?"

"I'm sorry for the intrusion," Edith said, "but I need to speak to Nurse Latham now."

"Now?" said Dr. Percy.

"I'm afraid so. I apologize, but something urgent's come up."

"It had better be urgent," said Dr. Percy.

"It can wait," said Maude. "I assure you, Dr. Percy."

"What?" said Dr. Percy. "What's going on here? For God's sake, make up your minds. No, no, that's all right. I'll make up your minds for you. Nurse Latham—go."

"But—"

"Go! And for God's sake," he added, his forehead flooding, "somebody mop me."

In the scrub room, Edith was waiting for Maude, her mask down.

"Well?" she said when Maude entered from the operating room.

"Well?" Maude echoed, pulling her own mask down from her mouth.

"What are you thinking?" Edith said. "I woke up and saw that your nurse's uniform wasn't on the hanger where you usually leave it. At first I thought you'd bizarrely decided to wear it when you went into London to see Stephen. I thought maybe you'd dressed in your uniform as a way to show him what you've done without him— who you've become. And then I realized. You didn't go." Edith crossed her arms. "What happened, Maude? Couldn't you bring yourself to see Stephen again?"

"No, I could do that," said Maude.

"So why didn't you?"

"For a very simple reason," Maude said. "Because I chose not to. *I* chose not to. *Me.*" She laughed lightly. "I lay awake for a long time last night, Edith. At first it didn't even occur to me not to go. Why shouldn't I, after all?"

"Indeed."

"Indeed," Maude repeated. "Either Stephen wants me back or for some reason he wants to explain in person why he left me. Either-or, right?"

"I suppose."

"Well, don't you see? Either way, it's what *he* wants. It's only because of some desire of his, or some need of his, or, or, or some I-don't-even-know-what of his that he and I would be getting together. And then I had to ask myself: What about me?"

Edith raised her face slightly, stuck out her chin, as if trying to formulate a response but was unable to.

"What do *I* want?" Maude went on slowly. "Do you know that in all the years since I got that note from Stephen, I've never tried to think of a way to contact him? *Not once.* I mean, why would I want to be with a man who didn't want to be with me? Really, Edith, ask yourself that."

"Yes, well, I'm sure your stand is quite admirable, and that all of us women could take a lesson from you. But what you seem to be forgetting is that some of us don't have the luxury of saying no."

But Maude was shaking her head. She'd heard this line of argument from Edith for years, on any number of occasions. The loss of Edith's husband, Ned Waterstone, was unfathomable, of course, the erasure of such a young and vital and promising life an unspeakable abomination of war.

And on many occasions, Maude had listened to Edith as she invoked that loss,
that personal tragedy, to help Maude put
some concern of her own into perspective.
Maude had listened to Edith, had held
Edith as she wept, had agreed with her.
But not this time.

"Edith," Maude said, reaching for her
friend's arms, to hold her or to hug her or
to give her whatever physical comfort she
craved, but Edith turned away from her.
Maude watched helplessly as Edith's
shoulders began to shake. "Edith, dear, do
you really want me to go to Stephen because you can't go to Ned?"

"Yes." Edith turned back toward Maude,
her eyes inflamed and wild. "Yes, that's exactly what I want. I want you to go to
Stephen for me, because I can't go to Ned.
I want you to go to Stephen for every
woman who can't go to the man she's lost
in war. For every wife, lover, mother, and
child."

"Well, I'm sorry, I can't do that," Maude
said softly, backing away from Edith. "I
don't mean to sound thoughtless, because
I'm not being thoughtless. In fact, I've
given this a great deal of thought, Edith.

Ned didn't have a choice. Stephen did. That's the difference. Stephen *chose* not to be with me."

"And so you can't forgive him?" Edith's voice was tight, angry.

"Yes," Maude answered. "Yes, I can."

"Then go."

"I can't. I won't."

"But why not?" Edith's voice was breaking, as if the strain, the effort, of trying to convince Maude might actually crack her.

"Because I don't love him anymore."

At that moment, one of the other nurses from the operating theater entered the room. She started to say something to Maude about Dr. Percy wanting to know when she was planning to grace the surgery with her presence. But after one look at the scene that confronted her—Edith and Maude breathing heavily, weeping, sagging, both barely able to stand—she stopped herself, retreating back into the operating theater. After she was gone, both Edith and Maude took a moment to collect themselves, smoothing their uniforms, brushing their cheeks with the backs of their hands. Edith was the first to speak again.

"I don't believe it, you know. About you not loving Stephen anymore. You loved him once—"

"That wasn't love."

"What?" Edith said. "What possibly can you mean?"

Edith stared at her with a completely blank expression, as though she had absolutely no idea of what Maude meant.

"That wasn't love. That was an *idea* of love that doesn't exist."

There was a long, drawn-out pause, as though Edith was gathering her words carefully, pulling them together to form something slightly delicate and difficult to express. "What happened," said Edith, "to the woman who used to sit around the nurses' station reading an ancient volume of Romantic poetry?"

"That woman is gone. And in her place is a woman who does cryptic puzzles, or hadn't you noticed?" Maude was aware that her own voice was bitter, but she went on. *Soldiered on,* she thought to herself. "Look, Edith," she said, "I appreciate your concern and all, but back then when Stephen and I first 'fell in love,' or whatever you want to call it, I suppose I was just kidding myself."

"Then I must have been kidding myself about Ned," said Edith coldly.

"I didn't say that."

"You didn't have to," Edith said.

"You misunderstand me," said Maude. "I'm so sorry, Edith, I didn't mean it. Wait, *no,*" she went on. "I did mean it."

"You did?"

Maude nodded. "Because I've often thought that we were all kidding ourselves. None of us is the same as we used to be before the war. That's life. Think how young we were! The memory that you have of Ned is who he was then, and that's wonderful. But that's not who he would have become. We don't know who he would have become."

Edith was staring at Maude in a frightening way. "Then," Edith began slowly, her eyes narrowing, "you don't know who Stephen has become either, do you?"

"No, well, I suppose I don't."

"What do you think Stephen wanted to say to you today that was so important and secret and all that?"

"I told you, Edith. Either—"

"I know, I know. Either, or. Either he wants you back or he wants to explain why he left you, right?"

Maude didn't answer. Suddenly she felt extremely tired, as though she'd actually fought in this war instead of simply nursed those who had. In all honesty, she was confused by the way that Stephen had sent a wounded soldier to her to convey messages.

"You don't know, do you?" Edith pressed on. She reached for her mask and raised it over her mouth. When she continued speaking, her voice came out sounding distant and muffled, but the message came through loud and clear. All Maude needed to see were Edith's eyes, still narrow, still red, still fierce. "I'm going into that operating room now to take your place. And you're getting on the next train to London. And do you know why? Because you don't know what Stephen is going to say. You can't know, not for certain. And the Maude Latham I know goes wherever she needs to go precisely *because* she doesn't know what she'll find there. She crosses oceans. She falls in love with her tutor. She stays in England in wartime. Unless," she went on, crossing the room, "you're telling me that *that* Maude is gone too. And if that's the case—well, I don't know that I could bear it." Edith backed against the double doors leading into the operating theater. "Because I've already seen enough casualties of war for one lifetime," she said, and she was gone.

It was still there.

Maude had been avoiding the Rose and Stag for more than five years now. Whenever she had come to London since her last visit with Stephen, she'd managed to bypass the tiny road off Waterloo Station that led to the front door of the pub and inn. At first she hadn't even realized she was avoiding it. Back when she still lived in Oxford and occasionally took the train into London, she would arrive at the station and then, without even thinking why, proceed to the exit opposite the one that would lead her to the Rose and Stag. One day, though, she'd found herself, out of habit, falling in with the crowd that was leaving the station by her old route. Then she saw the flower peddler's stand, the blossoms and sprays spilling across the pavement. She stopped. Even if a man hadn't barged into her, hard, from behind, the handle of his umbrella landing in the small of her back, Maude might have been thrown off balance in that moment. It was the feeling of having made a wrong turn. And then she realized that the turn she'd taken was "wrong" only if she wanted to avoid the Rose and Stag.

Which at first made no sense. After all, at that time she was still Stephen's lover—or at least she was as far as she knew. But why would a route that would take her right past the inn where the two of them had spent so many memorable hours be "wrong"? Maybe because they'd spent so many memorable hours there, she figured. Maybe because it would be too painful to revisit the site of such happy memories, to be reminded so pointedly of her lover's absence. But this morning, when Maude turned a corner and saw the familiar shingle hanging over the sidewalk and the century-old building rising behind it, the sensation that washed over her was neither the dread nor the pleasure she had thought she might experience in that moment, but relief. The Rose and Stag was somehow still standing.

And then all at once she knew: the reason she'd been avoiding it through all these years of war wasn't because she had been afraid to see it again, but because she had been afraid *not* to see it again. She had been afraid she would *never* see it again.

She pulled open the heavy door to the entrance of the inn and remembered its ridiculous weight. She walked into the dim lobby and remembered its mustiness as well as its tidiness. She approached the registration counter and remembered the old man sitting there. But he wasn't there. A young woman was there now, reading a magazine and twirling a curl of her hair.

"Excuse me," Maude said, and the woman looked up.

"Didn't hear you come in," said the young woman.

"There used to be a man here. The owner, I believe."

The woman looked at Maude, not knowing what she wanted.

"This was years ago," Maude said.

"Well, I mean, I was wondering. He didn't—in the war—"

"Oh, goodness me, no. He's right in there," she went on, nodding toward the doorway into the pub. "It's just all the young men what used to work in the pub ain't here no more."

"Oh, of course."

"So he moved over to the pub, and he asked me—I'm his niece—he asked me to help out."

"Oh, right. Thanks. By the way—"

The young woman looked up at Maude expectantly, still playing with a thread of hair. But Maude didn't know what to ask. She'd been summoned to the Rose and Slag, and after some deliberation she'd answered the summons. But now what?

Where was she to meet Stephen? Surely not in a room upstairs, and most assuredly not in "their" room, on the top floor, the one with the grapevine bedspread and the alcove overlooking the street. Under the circumstances, such an arrangement would be in the poorest of taste. In the lobby, then? Well, perhaps—but Stephen wasn't here.

And then she knew. Maude turned away

from the reservations clerk without so much as a thank-you. She crossed the narrow rug in the narrow entrance of the inn and faced the double door leading into the pub. From the far side of the frosted green glass came light chatter and little clatters. She reached forward, hesitated a moment, and then pushed.

The scene that opened before her captured exactly what the noises from the other side of the door had suggested, the same scene she'd encountered the first time she'd walked through that door, five years earlier, on the arm of Stephen Kendall: a lunchtime pub crowd.

"Mrs. Wick, isn't it?"

Maude, startled, turned toward the voice. She hadn't thought of that name in years, but the moment she heard it, she knew it applied to her. She couldn't help responding to it. She turned, and there he was—the old man who used to be behind the counter in the lobby. He was standing behind the bar now, pulling a pint but looking past the grand brass curve of the beer spigot, toward her.

"Yes," Maude heard herself say, felt herself smile. "Yes, I am." She was amazed that he remembered.

"It's good to see you again, it is," he said. He placed the filled glass on the bar top and pushed it toward a customer, who laid down a couple of coins and turned away.

"And you, too, Mr.—" Maude said, then stopped. "You know, I'm afraid I never knew your name."

He waved the question away with a dishrag. "It don't matter. What's in a name? It's the faces we need to know"—he leaned closer—"and I never forget a face." He straightened again. "The wife always told me to mind me own business, but it's a talent is what it is, to recall a face after all these years."

" 'Told'?" Maude said.

"Ay." His eyes flashed downward, briefly, then back up to Maude. "In the blitz, I lost her."

"I'm so sorry."

He placed a pint of ale before Maude. Apparently he'd remembered her usual order too. She began to fumble in her pocketbook, but the old man told her not to bother, in honor of such a grand occasion as her return to this establishment.

"And your husband?" he went on. "Mr. Wick?"

"Have you—have you seen him?" Maude asked. She knew what he meant by the question: Was "Mr. Wick" still alive? But Maude found she suddenly no longer had the patience for the nuances of this conversation. She wanted an answer, and she wanted it now.

"Me? Seen him?"

"I thought he might be here," Maude said.

The old man shook his head. "Not in here. Haven't had any reservations for a Mr. Wick over in the inn, neither."

"What about Kendall?"

The old man regarded her, cocking his head to one side. "Reservations for Kendall, you mean?" he said.

She nodded.

The old man continued to consider her, trying to make sense of the question. "No, no Kendall here," he said, and then, uncertainly, he moved away from Maude, down the bar, nodding to other customers to ask what their pleasure was.

Maude lifted the pint glass and moved away from the conversation into the crowd, as if sleepwalking. The entire day, she realized, was starting to acquire a somnambular haze. From the moment she'd opened her eyes, full of fresh resolve not to journey into London to meet Stephen, through her preparation in the operating theater for the appendectomy, to the argument with Edith in the scrub room; and then from the selection of the plainest clothes for, yes, the journey into London to meet Stephen, through the train trip past the suburban redbrick houses with black stovepipe chimneys, row upon row of houses that would have been identical if some of them hadn't been reduced to rubble, and now to the experience of discovering that the Rose and Stag and at least some of its denizens had survived the war, at least so far: Maude, lying awake in her cot the previous evening, had known to anticipate anything on such a day as this, but what she could have actually predicted of it was *nothing.*

Wasn't that the point? Wasn't that the very virtue that Edith had said she treasured in Maude—a willingness to go wherever life led her precisely *because* she never knew what she might find?

Maude found a seat at the window in the pub and glanced back at the old man behind the spigots and thought: Who knew she cared? Her relief at learning the old man was still alive was *absurd*—wasn't it? Maude didn't really know him. The world, London, Brackett-on-Heath were full of people whom Maude had never known and who had never known Maude and who were dead now, and there was nothing you could do about it, so you didn't, and you didn't even think about it much after a while. A fifteen-year-old boy who learned to identify the peculiar squeak of your shoes came and went, and you tried not to think about it, and you even succeeded. The husband of your best friend came and went, and you did think about it—think about it a lot, every day—and then, one day, you didn't.

But the nameless clerk behind the counter at an inn in the center of London? Maude couldn't say if she'd ever really thought of him to begin with, even before everyone's life became imperiled by the war. In any case, she hadn't thought of him in years. If Maude hadn't come here today at Stephen's behest, not only could she have gone the rest of her life without knowing if this nameless old man was alive or dead, but she also very likely would have gone the rest of her life without ever thinking of him again. He'd be alive, or he wouldn't, and she'd be none the wiser. But suddenly, to her surprise, once Maude walked through the entrance of the inn he was back in her life—or he wasn't. And then she *had* to know.

And now she knew: He was alive.

It was his wife who wasn't. Had Maude ever even met her? She closed her eyes, strained to remember. In all the times that she and Stephen had registered at the Rose and Stag, their room had always been waiting, immaculate. Maude recalled the rose that had lain across the bed on the occasion of their first visit. Always the linens were fresh, the pillows plumped, the window open, to catch the stray breeze and push the sheer curtains apart and aside and aloft. All those delicate preparations had been the doing of the unseen wife of the nameless proprietor, and now she was gone.

It was silly to mourn her, wasn't it? Or was it? For five years everybody had faced the same choice. Mourn everything worth mourning, in which case your life essentially ended, because there was simply too much to mourn. Or mourn nothing. Maude opened her eyes and sipped her ale and surveyed the crowd in the pub at the Rose and Stag. So many faces. So many lives. How could you even begin to mourn properly the losses they each had suffered— they all had suffered? Where to start?

The unseen wife of the nameless proprietor at an inn in the center of London, she supposed.

Maude closed her eyes again and turned away from the bar, toward the window; turned away from the window, toward the bar; turned away; and turned away; and turned away.

"Mrs. Wick?"

She turned. It was the old nameless man again, out from behind the bar, wiping her table with a dishcloth.

"I couldn't help noticing . . . ," he began.

Maude wiped her eyes.

"I mean, it's none of my business—" he started again.

"No, no, please," Maude said.

"But I couldn't help noticing, you seem in some . . . distress, you might say—"

"It's nothing," she said, smiling, shaking her head, looking down at her pint glass. "Thank you, anyway. I'm just waiting for someone. Mr. Wick," she added.

"Ah, I'm sure he'll turn up. Don't you fret."

"Thank you. You're very kind."

"Perhaps there's just been a misunderstanding."

It had occurred to Maude, of course. Occurred to her and then been dismissed by her. After all, what else could the puzzle clues from Stephen have meant? Yet what she said to the old man now was this: "There always is."

There always is a misunderstanding. There always is another interpretation. Five years earlier, Maude had decided to apply her intellectual powers to the study of Romantic poetry—to divining a meaning from tissues of verse a hundred years old. She thought now of the conversation she'd had with Helena at Harrods; the conversations she'd had with Lieutenant Jared Thomson in the hospital; the puzzle clues themselves that had led her back to this pub on this day; even the poem that she thought she understood so well, until she'd seen it torn apart, disemboweled as thoroughly as any building suffering a direct hit in the blitz, and the words that had always seemed to her redolent of romantic love suddenly stank of abandonment—a cruel lesson in reality: all of it, everything, nothing more than one misunderstanding after another.

"Yes, well, anyway," the old man went on, "it's nearly two-thirty. We'll be closing the kitchen soon. If you want to order lunch, now's the time."

"No, thank you," Maude said. Then she said it again, with some alarm: "No. Two-thirty, did you say? No. Oh, no."

Maude got up from the stool, grabbed her coat, and rushed past the old man. Unless she missed her guess, she knew where she would find Stephen Kendall.

CHAPTER NINE

He wasn't there.

Maude paused outside the pub and stared at the sidewalk opposite. She stared hard, studying the face of anyone who might bear the slightest resemblance to the Stephen Kendall she carried in her memory, because who knew how much the war had changed him? But if she were correct, she was half an hour late now, and had no right to expect to find him there, in front of the tobacconist's directly opposite the Rose and Stag, nor there, farther down the block in front of the fruiterer, nor there, at the corner, in front of the flower peddler.

But *there*—turning the corner, disappearing into Waterloo Station? Was that him? At this distance, in this state of mind, Maude might be imagining. She'd caught only a glimpse of a long gray overcoat, the back of a head. She couldn't be sure— couldn't be sure at all. She could probably convince herself of anything at the moment. Still, there was something, wasn't there—something about the slope of the shoulder, the shade of the hair, that made her wonder whether the presence she'd seen was one so powerfully familiar to her memory that all she needed to recognize it was a simple glimpse from a distance.

As Edith might have reminded her, there was only one way to find out.

Maude began to run. She ran down one sidewalk, then out into traffic, dodging a taxi, and over to the other side of the road. But when she turned the corner into the railway station, she stopped.

Where was he? Where was Stephen—or at least the man she thought might be him? Everywhere she looked, she saw coats—gray coats, and shoulders, and the backs of heads. Crowds of coats, pouring toward a platform, squeezing through a gate. She looked up, at the departure board, helplessly raking its lists of names and times, as if they might hold the answer. And no doubt they did—if only she

knew where Stephen was heading. But unlike the cryptic puzzles from the past three
days that she'd laid out on her cot the previous evening, the hidden meaning in this
current blur of words eluded her. She
didn't know where Stephen had come
from, didn't know where he'd be returning
to, didn't know anything about Stephen today except that he'd told her where to
meet him—had given her the necessary
clue after all—and now she'd missed him.
She'd been staring right at the answer for
three days running, and she had been too
blind to see it.

She could search every platform. That
was it. That was what she would do,
Maude told herself as she began to drift
toward one end of the terminal, bumping
past strangers, staggering almost, trying
not to appear like some mad rag woman of
the streets. Start at one end of Waterloo
Station, work her way toward the other.
That was her best shot, her only chance,
her—

"Maude."

She turned.

Stephen.

He was there. Stephen Kendall stood

before Maude, and for a moment she thought she might cry. He was changed, of course, as everyone had been by the war. His pale hair had something gray in it now, something *faded,* and his eyes seemed shadowed, and he held a cane in his hand. But still, indisputably, it was him. She had come so far this morning, had waited so long this afternoon, had come so close, sitting in the Rose and Stag, biding her time, only to lose him again, to miss him by mere seconds, that she found herself struggling not to break down in sobs of relief and release.

But then she remembered what he'd done to her.

"Stephen."

She straightened her back and extended her hand. "Good to see you," she said.

He looked at her for a moment. "Good to see you too," he finally said, and she saw that in order to take her hand he had to fuss with the cane, to move it from one hand to the other.

"Oh, Stephen," she said, before she knew it.

"It's all right. An old injury. I'm used to it

by now. I imagine you've encountered far worse at Brackett-on-Heath."

This was true. Maude had seen monstrous examples of carnage—of what damage humankind could wreak on itself if only it put the full force of its ingenuity to the task. But an injury to Stephen seemed somehow different to Maude. Intimate, even if the two of them no longer were. Maude knew what that right leg, now stiff, once looked like. She knew its smooth contours, skin rippling over muscle and bone, or the fine curls of its hair. She recalled the quick clip at which Stephen Kendall would walk across the courtyards of Oxford, late for a class or lost in thought, his robes billowing behind him. And now those days were over. The skin had ripped, the gait had slowed. Stephen Kendall would never be that blazing young man again, and in that moment in Waterloo Station Maude recalled something else Edith had said to her—about how one additional casualty of war can suddenly seem one too many.

"I'm sorry," Maude said. "I've made you feel self-conscious about your injury."

"Actually, I hardly give it a thought any-more," Stephen answered, smiling.

Maude remembered that smile now—its shy, tentative quality. The face to which that smile belonged was older than the one that she could conjure from memory. But age hadn't damaged his looks; on the con-trary, Maude might have thought that it ac-centuated Stephen's appearance, that it endowed him with *gravity,* if only she were still interested in such matters.

"Do you know I almost missed you to-day?" she said in what sounded like a mat-ter-of-fact manner. "I didn't realize until it was almost too late that 'fourteen across' in cryptic after cryptic after cryptic actually meant fourteen o'clock, *across* from the Rose and Stag." She paused. "Why did you have me meet you across from it? Why not inside?"

"I thought it sounded more clever," he said. "More dramatic. More worthy of Slay-ton." He paused and said, "I thought you didn't want to see me. I wouldn't have been surprised if you hadn't shown up. I didn't know what to think when Thomson told me your reaction to my letter." He glanced away. "How upset you looked that day."

"Oh?" Maude had no idea what to make of this remark of Stephen's. "And how exactly did you expect me to look? You'd made your intentions clear."

"Indeed, I thought I had," Stephen said. "And you rejected them."

"Me? Reject *your* intentions?" she said. "I would think it was the other way around, wouldn't you?"

"I'm afraid I don't follow." He blinked once and looked back at her.

"Really, Stephen, if you'd wanted to tell me you didn't love me anymore, why use the very poem that once meant so much to us?"

"What?"

"Why pervert its meaning in such a manner?" she went on, overriding him. "Oh, I suppose I should be grateful. If you'd wanted to snap me out of my little romantic fantasy of what a life with Stephen Kendall would be like, then that was the way to do it, all right. Do you know something?" Maude unclasped her pocketbook and began rooting around inside it. Stephen reached into the inside breast pocket of his jacket and produced a handkerchief, but Maude shook her head. "It's not tissues I'm looking for. I'm not crying. You'd be surprised how long it's been since I've cried, Stephen. I suppose I should be grateful to you for that too. You, and the war."

"Maude, really, I'm at a loss here." He stuffed his ineffective square of white cloth back in his pocket.

"Ah, here it is."

From her pocketbook Maude produced an envelope. Even in the gray indoor light of an overcast afternoon in London, it looked yellowed.

Stephen stared at it for a moment, leaning hard on his cane. "Is this what I think it is?" he said then, reaching for it with his free hand.

"I know, it's pathetic," Maude said, relinquishing the envelope to Stephen, "the rejected suitor walking around with the kiss-off letter after all these years. But I assure you I'm not still carrying it for sentimental reasons. Quite the contrary. There were times these past few years when I would find myself alone at night in my cot in the nurses' quarters, and do you know what I would do, Stephen? I would look at this letter because it *helped* me. It actually helped me remember what I once thought love was, and what I had learned it isn't. This was when I was seeing Allen Drake," she added, "a surgeon at Brackett-on-Heath."

This last remark seemed to have the desired effect. Stephen glanced up from the pages of the letter, a slightly pained expression crossing his brow, deepening the lines on his face. Maude waited.

"Something's missing," he said. He looked down at the two pages of the letter, one in each hand, then up at Maude again.

"I should say there is," she said. "Most of the poem by A. L. Slayton. All but the last stanza."

"That's what I mean, Maude." Stephen glanced around suddenly with obvious agitation. "I need to sit."

"Oh," Maude said. "Oh. Of course."

Stephen pointed with his cane toward a bench on one side of the concourse. Maude knew from her training as a nurse not to offer to help patients with a disability unless they requested it. Let them make their own way in the world until they'd reached their limits. Then and only then, when they wanted you to, when a patient turned to you with a mildly beckoning—but not yet beseeching—outstretched palm, were you to step in and offer your assistance. And so the two of them progressed now across the concourse, parting a path through the crowd, Stephen moving stiffly, Maude slowly, observing his pace in order to stay at his side. And as they did so, she couldn't help thinking of the first time the two of them had walked through this station. In those days they had moved arm in arm as one, and swiftly. Unencumbered. Unafraid for once to communicate to the world that they were lovers. Youthful lovers, no less. Now, their forward movement suggested nothing so much as a premonition of how they would seem as an elderly couple. Not that they were going to be an elderly couple, of course—and not that Stephen's sudden exhaustion in this moment, Maude suspected, had as much to do with his injury as with something he'd seen in the letter.

Maude sat beside him and waited.

"Do you know," he said after a long moment, both hands resting atop the handle

of his cane, the letter he'd routed to her
through the graces of Lieutenant Thomson
some five years earlier sticking out from his
hand like some sort of afterthought, "we
look as if we should be passing information to each other?"

"I don't know what you mean," she said.

"The two of us, sitting side by side, in a
railway station. You've no idea how often
I've enacted this exact scenario over the
past few years."

"In naval intelligence?" Maude said,
leaning back.

"You knew?" He turned his head slightly
toward her.

"I'd like to pretend that it was my brilliant
intuition, but in fact it was Helena who told
me," she admitted.

Stephen looked away again. He tapped
his cane on the concrete floor of the railway station, tapped it again, tapped,
tapped, tapped it.

"A code?" she said.

He emitted a quick, sharp laugh. "No.
Nerves, actually," he added. "You see, I've
saved something of yours over the years
too."

Stephen reached into his inside jacket pocket and handed her a small parcel.

"Oh, no," Maude said. She accepted the package, unfolded the brown paper, peeling back a corner until she saw the familiar, faded cover of the collected poems of A. L. Slayton. Maude stared at him. "But this can't be my copy."

Stephen nodded. "It is."

"But I don't understand. *How?* I threw this away years ago."

"Lieutenant Thomson," Stephen said. "He watched you toss it in a trash can."

"He was there?" Maude said, remembering how she'd gone into the staff lounge that day. But of course; earlier, she'd told Jared Thomson that there was hot tea waiting in the lounge, and so he was still there in a corner of the room, unnoticed, when she came in to throw the book into the dustbin. He'd seen everything and had waited until she had left the room again, and he'd then retrieved it.

"He thought it might have some meaning for me," said Stephen. "And it did. I just didn't know what until now."

"Now? What's happened now?"

"The letter," he said, turning toward her.

"The thing is, Maude, I sent you the entire poem. Not just the final stanza."

"What do you mean?"

"I wrote out the whole poem for you. And before I did that, in the same letter, I wrote you an explanation that even though I had no choice but to return briefly to Oxford in order to speed my recovery from my injury, I would still find a way to be with you when the war was over. And I said I loved you as much as ever." He turned away from Maude again and banged the ball of his cane against the concrete. The surprisingly sharp crack of wood on concrete rose above the dull roar of the crowd moving this way and that, and echoed throughout Waterloo Station.

The evenness of Maude's voice offered a counterpoint to his dramatic gesture. "What exactly are you saying, Stephen?" she said in almost a whisper.

"I'm saying that a *page is missing from the letter.* The middle page. I can't explain it except to say that Helena must have removed it. I always suspected her of going through my things, but I was never able to catch her. And I was so heavily medicated during my recovery, it's entirely possible that she helped herself to my outgoing mail."

Maude sat on the bench, not moving. Edith was right again. She'd told Maude she couldn't know what Stephen was going to say. As it turned out, even *Stephen* couldn't possibly have known what he was going to say until he'd seen the letter again.

"Ever since I heard from Lieutenant Thomson how you'd reacted to my note," Stephen went on, "and mind you, he had no idea of the contents, but since then I've been desperate to get in touch with you. The strict security considerations in my unit always prevented me. It was only after we launched the Normandy invasion and my immediate mission was over that I could send poor in-the-dark Thomson back to you."

"What do you mean?" she asked. "He was injured. Shock."

"We all have shock, to a certain degree," Stephen said, smiling grimly. "I'm afraid Lieutenant Thomson was on an intelligence mission of another kind. To find out whether you were willing to see me again. That was all he was told to do. The rest of it was kept from him—and by 'the rest of it' I mean the part where I get to hear from you myself why you no longer love me."

"But I do," Maude said before she knew what she was saying, and then she let herself move against him, let herself cry while he held her and kissed her face, her hair, her mouth.

"Oh, my darling," he was saying, and in a moment he was crying too, and they were talking in a flurry of words, and laughing and whispering, making up for all these years apart, or at least trying to as best they possibly could.

"Do you remember the first time we were here in London?" she asked him a little while later, when the crying had stopped and they were simply sitting together, touching, holding. "The war was only a possibility then."

"Yes," he answered softly.

"It seems so long ago."

"Yes."

"And now the war is almost over."

"Nearly so, I hope."

She buried her face in his jacket. "What's going to happen to us?" she asked.

"What do you mean?"

"How can any of us go back to the life we had before the war? We can't get it back, not really."

"No, I suppose not," said Stephen.

"It will never be the way it was."

"It will be something else," he said.

Maude lifted her head and saw the people rushing through the station, saw other couples meet and kiss, saw hellos and good-byes, and took note of the incessant churn and pulse of life. They would have something else now; he was right. It was impossible to return to a time that no longer existed, to a world that had changed. Those two people were gone now, that young Oxford tutor and his American student, those two innocents who loved each other in the best way that they knew how. But here, in their place, were a man and a woman no less in love, tired, tear-stained, grateful beyond expression, sitting together on a bench in Waterloo Station—sitting in the *waiting* room—Maude realized, smiling slightly, for that was in fact what they were doing now after all this time. They were waiting, together, for the rest of life to begin.

CHAPTER TEN

By the time Maude Kendall finished telling her granddaughter everything, the light inside the attic had grown bluish and dim. It was late afternoon now, almost evening. She and Carrie had come here today in order to purge this place of unnecessary objects, and instead they had gotten sidetracked by Maude's extraordinary story. When she was done speaking, neither woman said anything for a while. Then, finally, Carrie asked in a small voice, "So I guess real love—love without irony, love without withholding—isn't just a fantasy."

"Oh no, my dear, it's not," said Maude. "Why, did you really think it was?"

Carrie shifted uneasily in her seat, and then she told her grandmother all about her boyfriend, Rufus Cowley, the drummer, and how she didn't feel very much for him. "I started thinking that I should just accept him. That maybe this is what love feels like. After all, he's perfectly nice and interesting and good to me, and he's extremely sexy too, Grandma."

"Sounds a bit like Allen Drake," said Maude, smiling. "The thing is, love is an element whose chemical makeup is unknown. No one knows why two people meet each other and then feel an intensity that overshadows everything else in their lives. A. L. Slayton and all the Romantic poets understood that such a love is mysterious, but that when it happens, it should be revered. What I'm trying to tell you, dear, in this terribly long-winded way," she said, "is that there *is* such a thing as an ideal love, and that you of all people, my darling girl, shouldn't ask for anything less. You're a marvelous girl. And you're young. And when you go off next week, the world will open to you like . . . well, like an oyster." She laughed. "I've never been much of a poet myself," she said. "I leave that to other people."

Maude Kendall might not have been a poet, but she knew a great deal about poetry, and in fact she and her husband, Stephen, had both taught literature to- gether at the University of Sussex in En- gland after the war. They couldn't stay on in Oxford because Helena, who had finally agreed to a divorce, would have been an uncomfortable presence. So they rented a small cottage in Sussex, where they lived for many years before coming to the States. First they moved to New York City, both of them teaching poetry classes at Columbia University, and then, when Stephen reached retirement age, they de- cided to move back upstate to Longwood Falls, the town where Maude had grown up, and which she was finally able to ap- preciate after so many years of unasked- for excitement.

Longwood Falls, in 1974, was much as Maude had remembered it. Of course, by now her parents were dead, but her brother and sister both still lived in the area with their children, and she and Stephen and their daughter, Louisa—Carrie's mother—made a peaceful and satisfying small-town life for themselves. And here they'd stayed ever since, their life full of grown children and teenage grandchildren and friends, their love never dying, never even fading, their devotion to each other apparent to anyone who walked by their house on a summer evening and saw Maude and Stephen Kendall sitting together on their front porch glider swing, arms entwined.

But though their love didn't flicker for an instant, they both grew old, and frail, all of which was to be expected, Maude knew, and which she could accept in herself, but which still was shocking when it came to Stephen. Sometimes, in those final months of his life, she would look over at him when he was sleeping beside her, and she would see how thin he'd become, his hair still wavy but now entirely gray and lank. And his face, which had been so handsome and boyish throughout much of his life, had finally changed sharply, his mouth drooping at the corners from the weight of his illness, the lines deepened in his brow. In sleep he appeared troubled, as though he were working out a particularly challenging math problem. He was a very old man. It was unbelievable to Maude that this had happened to *him.*

Forever, in her mind, he was the young,

exuberant Oxford tutor, an ardent young man with a strong, compact body that she'd loved to touch. They'd both been so young before the war aged everyone prematurely. If only—if only she could go back to that time, that *innocence.* But you couldn't go back, no one could; everyone, at some point or other, had to face that astonishing fact in their lives. And if they were lucky enough to have loved someone the way she and Stephen had loved each other for nearly sixty-three years, then it would be all the more terrible when it was time to say good-bye.

Maude knew, from her years of nursing, that Stephen was dying. She didn't even have to be told by the family doctor who had been their physician since they moved back to Longwood Falls. She knew simply by the changes in Stephen. He had had a full life and was ninety years old, yet how could Maude bear to say good-bye to him? Every night, the week before he died, she would come downstairs to the kitchen at about 3 A.M., unable to sleep. She'd sit at the table with a glass of water, looking out at the stars over the yard, and thinking of how he'd once left her, and then returned, but knowing that the next time he left her, which would be soon, it would be forever. He would disappear, but not to war, and there would be no point to waiting and hoping. Stephen would never return this time, never. The thought of it was so painful that every night, sitting in that kitchen, Maude wept quietly, crying into the sleeve of her bathrobe so she wouldn't wake him.

But one night, at 3 A.M., when Maude was sitting alone in the kitchen, she heard a creak on the stairs. And she looked up and there he was. He'd come downstairs all by himself, which he hadn't done in weeks.

"Stephen," Maude had said, astonished. "What are you doing up?"

"I woke up and you weren't in bed," he said. "I missed you."

"Well, sit down, sit down," she said, helping him into a chair.

"Thank you, my love," he said.

She poured him a glass of water too, and they sat together, looking out at the dark night, her hand on top of his, holding it, stroking it.

"What are you thinking about?" he asked.

Maude looked at him. "The scarf you lent me so long ago," she said. "Remember?"

He nodded. "Oh yes," he said. "I gave it to you to wear in the cold. And then Helena saw it and became suspicious. I remember."

"And remember our room at the Rose and Stag? The pattern on the bedspread?"

"Little grapes on vines," he said, "winding all the way down to the bottom." He sighed deeply, looking at Maude for a long time, as if trying to memorize her. *Don't memorize me,* she'd thought. *Take me with you instead.* What was the point of life if you weren't beside the one you loved? How could Maude Kendall go on without Stephen, her husband of so many years? It would be like losing a limb, she thought, and then she amended that: no, it would be like losing her heart. She didn't think she could bear it.

"You're crying," Stephen said, reaching out and touching her face.

"Oh, Stephen," Maude said, "I don't know how I can go on if you go away from me. I lived through that once, but this is different."

He leaned forward and kissed her face; his mouth was dry, parched. "My darling," he said in a slow, hesitant voice, "I won't go away. Or at least if I do, I won't be going very far." And then he became too weak, or too overcome with emotion himself, to continue speaking. She helped him back up to bed and then she lay beside him.

Maude wanted to feel Stephen against her; she knew he was going to go away from her very, very soon, and the past and the present came rushing at her with immense speed and force: Stephen and Maude in his study at Oxford, their heads tilting together in the fading light, or else the two of them lying in that bed in the Rose and Stag, his lean body against hers, his head tipped back in pleasure. And then their separation throughout the war, when she thought he no longer loved her, and the pain was unbearable, worse than anything. And then their life together, lived in Sussex and then the United States. And it had been quite a life, populated by friends and dinner tables and students and children and good music and long walks and quiet nights spent reading poetry aloud.

And love. Oh, love was everywhere throughout these years. It twined through their life like that grape pattern on that awful bedspread. A life was made up of small moments; that was all you got: a million snapshots of how things were, and then, a moment later, how they no longer were, and never would be again. But at least she'd had that with him. It had been full and rich and bracing; she'd embraced it, taken him into her in every way she knew how.

When she'd left this very town at age eighteen, she'd known nothing. "I want to know the world," a trembling young Maude had told the panel of Oxford trustees, and so she had. She'd gotten to know the world, the bad parts as well as the good, the shameful inhumanity that coexisted with decency. It was all there; Stephen had guided her through life. He'd tutored her, and she in turn had tutored him. She'd taught him it was possible to be happy. That a marriage could be loving and didn't have to be cold and spent in separate rooms.

And now it was time for all the lessons to end. "I have never loved anyone the way I love you," Stephen said that night. "You are still as you were the first time we met."

"And you are too," she said, realizing that it was true, that even through the masks of age that both of them were forced to wear, as though the end of life were like some cruel, strange Mardi Gras, young Stephen Kendall, her tutor, her lover, her husband, could be seen. That would never die. Her tears fell upon his face, and all over the blanket she'd pulled up around him so he would not be cold, for he chilled very easily lately. The tears fell and fell, and she said to him, "Oh, my Stephen, oh, my love, please don't leave me." She was begging him, as though he had a choice in the matter, as though he could do something about it. As though, because he was Stephen Kendall, the bravest and truest man she knew, he could actually stop time.

"It will be all right, my love," he said to her in a whisper. "It will be all right, I promise you. I won't be far away." And then he put his arms around her and dropped off to sleep against her. His breathing was even and soft, and she relaxed a bit, calmed herself down, but she didn't dare to sleep that night.

As the light started to touch the edges of the sky, Stephen Kendall died in his wife Maude's arms.

And now, telling all of this to her granddaughter Carrie, Maude felt the pain and suffering all over again. It was as though grief never ended, she thought. Why should she live without Stephen? What reason was there?

"You know," Carrie suddenly said, as though she had the ability to read people's minds, "today, as you've been telling me all these things I never knew, it's like you've conjured him up. I never knew him when he was alive as well as I do now. You haven't forgotten anything, Grandma. It's all stored inside you, and it's in perfect condition." She paused, then went on in a more measured voice. "This morning, when I first showed up to help you, you said that you didn't want to live a long time. That there was really no point to it. I know it's been very hard, I know you're sad a lot of the time. I know you miss him. I would give anything to have a life in which I loved someone the way you loved Grandpa Stephen. And if, one day, the man I loved died before I did, I guess I'd think it was . . . I don't know how to say this, it sounds so corny . . . but I guess I'd think it was my duty to stay here and remember him, and what we had together, and tell people about him. I'd tell everyone who would listen. Because that's one of the most incredible abilities any of us has, isn't it? The ability to remember."

Maude Kendall sat and looked at her young granddaughter. "Carrie," she said after a while, "how did you get so smart?"

"Good genes?" said Carrie.

"And you haven't even started out yet, really," said Maude.

"Two weeks from today I'm off," said Carrie. "But I'm not going by boat, like you did. I'm taking an airplane to London and then someone from the university is going to meet me and take me to St. Hilda's College, Oxford."

"I'm so glad you'll be there," said Maude. "I can't wait to hear what it's like now."

"I'm sure it's still wonderful," said Carrie.

"But no affairs with your tutors, please,"

said Maude. "These days, things are quite different, and I would feel a tutor might be taking advantage of a student. Better stick to someone your own age, all right?"

"All right," said Carrie, smiling. She thought for a moment. "Oh, I was wondering," she said. "Whatever happened to all the people you knew back then?"

"Let me see," said Maude. "Well, my dear friend Edith Drake, she still lives in England."

"Drake?" said Carrie, confused. "I thought her name was Waterstone. From her husband, Ned, the pilot who was killed."

"He was her *first* husband," Maude said. "And then, in 1946, she married Allen Drake. Believe me, it made me extraordinarily happy all around. She went to work for a children's hospital in London, and Allen had an extremely successful surgical practice. They both retired some years ago and live in Cornwall, by the sea, right near their son Ned's family."

"They named him Ned," said Carrie quietly. "That's so wonderful." She paused. "And how about Helena Kendall?"

Maude's face grew slightly tight. "She

died in the early fifties," she said. "Double pneumonia. She was fragile in every way. Though she was never able to really love Stephen in any meaningful sense, it was impossible for her to get over him. I still feel very bad about that. As soon as we heard she was so ill, Stephen went and stayed with her for a week. He was there at her bedside when she died."

"And what," asked Carrie finally, "about Lieutenant Jared Thomson?"

Her grandmother laughed fully. "Don't you know?" she asked.

"No, I don't."

"He's the famous stage actor Sir Jared Clark Thomson. Queen Elizabeth knighted him ten years ago."

"So when he came to your hospital and pretended to be in shock," said Carrie, "he really showed how talented he was."

"Exactly," said Maude. "When your grandfather and I lived in Sussex after the war, and Jared was appearing in a play in the West End, he'd always send us complimentary tickets. To this day he is a brilliant actor. In fact, he didn't know about your grandpa passing away, and just last week he sent me two tickets to see him play

King Lear in London in November. But of course I'm not going to go."

Carrie regarded her for a while. Then, in a quiet voice, she said, "I'd love to meet him. And London isn't very far from Oxford, where I'll be living. Hint, hint, Grandma."

"No, it's not possible," said Maude.

"But it is," said her granddaughter. "I think it's the best thing in the world."

Maude murmured protestations, but still she began to think: What *would* it be like to go back there, to see those old sights, without Stephen by her side? Would it be bearable, or would she be overcome with melancholy? It hadn't occurred to her to ever go back, for she'd thought it would have been too sad. She hadn't even considered accepting Sir Jared's tickets to see him play Lear, and yet now that Carrie had mentioned it, the idea of it stirred something inside her.

Sixty-three years ago she'd traveled across an ocean to meet the man she would love with all her heart for the rest of her life. And now maybe, just maybe, she would be crossing that ocean once again. She saw herself standing at a rail, looking out at the sea. And she knew, somehow,

that no matter where she went during the
rest of her days on earth, Stephen was
right; she heard his words in her head,
even now, heard him saying, *I won't be far
away.*